"Toni Morrison may be the last classic American writer, squarely in the tradition of Poe, Melville, Twain, and Faulkner." —*Newsweek*

"The finest novelist of our time." —*Vogue*

"She has an awesome lyric flair. . . . Morrison has the control of a skilled choreographer, with a careful eye pinned on pacing, suspense, grace, and frenzy." —*Charlotte Observer*

"One of the most exciting living American writers." —*Kansas City Star*

"Morrison is easily the finest writer on the contemporary scene." —*Philadelphia Bulletin*

"A writer of amazing skill." —*Roanoke Times & World*

TONI MORRISON was born in Lorain, Ohio. She is the author of five other novels, all available in Plume editions: *Sula, Song of Solomon,* which won the 1978 National Book Critics Circle Award for fiction, *Tar Baby, Beloved,* which won the 1988 Pulitzer Prize for fiction, and *Jazz.* The winner of the 1993 Nobel Prize in Literature, she is Robert F. Goheen Professor, Council of the Humanities, at Princeton University.

ALSO BY TONI MORRISON

Sula (1974)

Song of Solomon (1977)

Tar Baby (1981)

Beloved (1987)

Jazz (1992)

Playing in the Dark (1992)

Race-ing Justice, En-Gendering Power (1992)
Editor

The Nobel Lecture in Literature (1994)

Birth of a Nation'hood (1996)
Coeditor with Claudia Brodsky Lacour

The Dancing Mind (1996)

Paradise (1997)

Toni Morrison

THE
BLUEST
EYE

With a new Afterword by the author

A PLUME BOOK

PLUME
Published by the Penguin Group
Penguin Books USA Inc., 375 Hudson Street, New York, New York 10014, U.S.A.
Penguin Books Ltd, 27 Wrights Lane, London W8 5TZ, England
Penguin Books Australia Ltd, Ringwood, Victoria, Australia
Penguin Books Canada Ltd, 10 Alcorn Avenue, Toronto, Ontario, Canada M4V 3B2
Penguin Books (N.Z.) Ltd, 182–190 Wairau Road, Auckland 10, New Zealand

Penguin Books Ltd, Registered Offices: Harmondsworth, Middlesex, England

Published by Plume, an imprint of Dutton Signet, a division of Penguin Books USA Inc.
This is an authorized reprint of a hardcover edition published by Alfred A. Knopf.
Originally published by Holt, Rinehart and Winston, Inc, in 1970.
For information address Alfred A. Knopf, Inc.,
201 East 50th Street, New York, N.Y. 10022.

First Plume Printing, September, 1994

40 39 38 37

 REGISTERED TRADEMARK—MARCA REGISTRADA

LIBRARY OF CONGRESS CATALOGING-IN-PUBLICATION DATA
Morrison, Toni.
    The bluest eye / Toni Morrison, with a new afterword by the
author.
      p.   cm.
    ISBN 0-452-27305-6
    1. Afro-Americans—Ohio—Fiction.   2. Girls—Ohio—Fiction.
I. Title.
PS3563.O8749B55   1994
813'.54—dc20   94-14448
                                                    CIP

Printed in the United States of America

PUBLISHER'S NOTE
This is a work of fiction. Names, characters, places, and incidents either are the
product of the author's imagination or, are used fictitiously, and any resemblance
to actual persons, living or dead, events, or locales is entirely coincidental.

BOOKS ARE AVAILABLE AT QUANTITY DISCOUNTS WHEN USED TO PROMOTE PRODUCTS
OR SERVICES. FOR INFORMATION PLEASE WRITE TO PREMIUM MARKETING DIVISION,
PENGUIN BOOKS USA INC., 375 HUDSON STREET, NEW YORK, NEW YORK 10014.

To the two who gave me life
and the one who made me free

The Bluest Eye

Here is the house. It is green and white. It has a red door. It is very pretty. Here is the family. Mother, Father, Dick, and Jane live in the green-and-white house. They are very happy. See Jane. She has a red dress. She wants to play. Who will play with Jane? See the cat. It goes meow-meow. Come and play. Come play with Jane. The kitten will not play. See Mother. Mother is very nice. Mother, will you play with Jane? Mother laughs. Laugh, Mother, laugh. See Father. He is big and strong. Father, will you play with Jane? Father is smiling. Smile, Father, smile. See the dog. Bowwow goes the dog. Do you want to play with Jane? See the dog run. Run, dog, run. Look, look. Here comes a friend. The friend will play with Jane. They will play a good game. Play, Jane, play.

Here is the house it is green and white it has a red door it is very pretty here is the family mother father dick and jane live in the green-and-white house they are very happy see jane she has a red dress she wants to play who will play with jane see the cat it goes meow-meow come and play come play with jane the kitten will not play see mother mother is very nice mother will you play with jane mother laughs laugh mother laugh see father he is big and strong father will you play with jane father is smiling smile father smile see the dog bowwow goes the dog do you want to play do you want to play with jane see the dog run run dog run look look here comes a friend the friend will play with jane they will play a good game play jane play

Hereisthehouseitisgreenandwhiteithasareddooritisverypretty hereisthefamilymotherfatherdickandjaneliveinthegreenandw hitehousetheyareveryhappyseejaneshehasareddressshewants toplaywhowillplaywithjaneseethecatitgoesmeowmeowcomea ndplaycomeplaywithjanethekittenwillnotplayseemothermoth erisverynicemotherwillyouplaywithjanemotherlaughslaughm otherlaughseefatherheisbigandstrongfatherwillyouplaywithja nefatherissmilingsmilefathersmileseethedogbowwowgoesthe dogdoyouwanttoplaydoyouwanttoplaywithjaneseethedogrun rundogrunlooklookherecomesafriendthefriendwillplaywithja netheywillplayagoodgameplayjaneplay

Quiet as it's kept, there were no marigolds in the fall of 1941. We thought, at the time, that it was because Pecola was having her father's baby that the marigolds did not grow. A little examination and much less melancholy would have proved to us that our seeds were not the only ones that did not sprout; nobody's did. Not even the gardens fronting the lake showed marigolds that year. But so deeply concerned were we with the health and safe delivery of Pecola's baby we could think of nothing but our own magic: if we planted the seeds, and said the right words over them, they would blossom, and everything would be all right.

It was a long time before my sister and I admitted to ourselves that no green was going to spring from our seeds. Once we knew, our guilt was relieved only by fights and mutual accusations about who was to blame. For years I thought my sister was right: it was my fault. I had planted them too far down in the earth. It never occurred to either of us that the earth itself might have been unyielding. We had dropped our seeds in our own little plot of black dirt just as Pecola's father had dropped his seeds in his own plot of black dirt. Our innocence and faith were no more productive than his lust or despair. What is clear now is that of all of that hope, fear, lust, love, and grief, nothing remains but Pecola and the unyielding earth. Cholly Breedlove is dead; our innocence too. The seeds shriveled and died; her baby too.

There is really nothing more to say—except why. But since why is difficult to handle, one must take refuge in how.

Autumn

Nuns go by as quiet as lust, and drunken men and sober eyes sing in the lobby of the Greek hotel. Rosemary Villanucci, our next-door friend who lives above her father's café, sits in a 1939 Buick eating bread and butter. She rolls down the window to tell my sister Frieda and me that we can't come in. We stare at her, wanting her bread, but more than that wanting to poke the arrogance out of her eyes and smash the pride of ownership that curls her chewing mouth. When she comes out of the car we will beat her up, make red marks on her white skin, and she will cry and ask us do we want her to pull her pants down. We will say no. We don't know what we should feel or do if she does, but whenever she asks us, we know she is offering us something precious and that our own pride must be asserted by refusing to accept.

School has started, and Frieda and I get new brown stockings and cod-liver oil. Grown-ups talk in tired, edgy voices about Zick's Coal Company and take us along in the evening to the railroad tracks where we fill burlap sacks with the tiny pieces of coal lying about. Later we walk home, glancing back to see the great carloads of slag being dumped, red hot and smoking, into the ravine that skirts the steel mill. The dying fire lights the sky with a dull orange glow. Frieda and I lag behind, staring at the patch of color surrounded by black. It is impossible not to feel a shiver when our feet leave the gravel path and sink into the dead grass in the field.

Our house is old, cold, and green. At night a kerosene lamp lights one large room. The others are braced in darkness, peopled by roaches and mice. Adults do not talk to us—they give us directions. They issue orders without providing information. When we trip and fall down they glance at us; if we cut or bruise ourselves, they ask us are we crazy. When we catch colds, they shake their heads in disgust at our lack of consideration. How, they ask us, do you expect anybody to get anything done if you all are sick? We cannot answer them. Our illness is treated with contempt, foul Black Draught, and castor oil that blunts our minds.

When, on a day after a trip to collect coal, I cough once, loudly, through bronchial tubes already packed tight with phlegm, my mother frowns. "Great Jesus. Get on in that bed. How many times do I have to tell you to wear something on your head? You must be the biggest fool in this town. Frieda? Get some rags and stuff that window."

Frieda restuffs the window. I trudge off to bed, full of guilt and self-pity. I lie down in my underwear, the metal in my black garters hurts my legs, but I do not take them off, for it is too cold to lie stockingless. It takes a long time for my body to heat its place in the bed. Once I have generated a silhouette of warmth, I dare not move, for there is a cold place one-half inch in any direction. No one speaks to me or asks how I feel. In an hour or two my mother comes. Her hands are large and rough, and when she rubs the Vicks salve on my chest, I am rigid with pain. She takes two fingers' full of it at a time, and massages my chest until I am faint. Just when I think I will tip over into a scream, she scoops out a little of the salve on her forefinger and puts it in my mouth, telling me to swallow. A hot flannel is wrapped about my neck and chest. I am covered up with heavy quilts and ordered to sweat, which I do—promptly.

Later I throw up, and my mother says, "What did you puke on the bed clothes for? Don't you have sense enough to hold your head out the bed? Now, look what you did. You think I got time for nothing but washing up your puke?"

The puke swaddles down the pillow onto the sheet—green-gray, with flecks of orange. It moves like the insides of an uncooked egg. Stubbornly clinging to its own mass, refusing to break up and be removed. How, I wonder, can it be so neat and nasty at the same time?

My mother's voice drones on. She is not talking to me. She is talking to the puke, but she is calling it my name: Claudia. She wipes it up as best she can and puts a scratchy towel over the large wet place. I lie down again. The rags have fallen from the window crack, and the air is cold. I dare not call her back and am reluctant to leave my warmth. My mother's anger humiliates me; her words chafe my cheeks, and I am crying. I do not know that she is not angry at me, but at my sickness. I believe she

despises my weakness for letting the sickness "take holt."
By and by I will not get sick; I will refuse to. But for
now I am crying. I know I am making more snot, but I
can't stop.

My sister comes in. Her eyes are full of sorrow. She
sings to me: "When the deep purple falls over sleepy
garden walls, someone thinks of me. . . ." I doze,
thinking of plums, walls, and "someone."

But was it really like that? As painful as I remember?
Only mildly. Or rather, it was a productive and
fructifying pain. Love, thick and dark as Alaga syrup,
eased up into that cracked window. I could smell
it—taste it—sweet, musty, with an edge of wintergreen in
its base—everywhere in that house. It stuck, along with
my tongue, to the frosted windowpanes. It coated my
chest, along with the salve, and when the flannel came
undone in my sleep, the clear, sharp curves of air
outlined its presence on my throat. And in the night,
when my coughing was dry and tough, feet padded into
the room, hands repinned the flannel, readjusted the
quilt, and rested a moment on my forehead. So when I
think of autumn, I think of somebody with hands who
does not want me to die.

It was autumn too when Mr. Henry came. Our roomer.
Our roomer. The words ballooned from the lips and
hovered about our heads—silent, separate, and pleasantly
mysterious. My mother was all ease and satisfaction in
discussing his coming.

"You know him," she said to her friends. "Henry
Washington. He's been living over there with Miss Della

Jones on Thirteenth Street. But she's too addled now to keep up. So he's looking for another place."

"Oh, yes." Her friends do not hide their curiosity. "I been wondering how long he was going to stay up there with her. They say she's real bad off. Don't know who he is half the time, and nobody else."

"Well, that old crazy nigger she married up with didn't help her head none."

"Did you hear what he told folks when he left her?"

"Uh-uh. What?"

"Well, he run off with that trifling Peggy—from Elyria. You know."

"One of Old Slack Bessie's girls?"

"That's the one. Well, somebody asked him why he left a nice good church woman like Della for that heifer. You know Della always did keep a good house. And he said the honest-to-God real reason was he couldn't take no more of that violet water Della Jones used. Said he wanted a woman to smell like a woman. Said Della was just too clean for him."

"Old dog. Ain't that nasty!"

"You telling me. What kind of reasoning is that?"

"No kind. Some men just dogs."

"Is that what give her them strokes?"

"Must have helped. But you know, none of them girls wasn't too bright. Remember that grinning Hattie? She wasn't never right. And their Auntie Julia is still trotting up and down Sixteenth Street talking to herself."

"Didn't she get put away?"

"Naw. County wouldn't take her. Said she wasn't harming anybody."

"Well, she's harming me. You want something to scare

the living shit out of you, you get up at five-thirty in the morning like I do and see that old hag floating by in that bonnet. Have mercy!"

They laugh.

Frieda and I are washing Mason jars. We do not hear their words, but with grown-ups we listen to and watch out for their voices.

"Well, I hope don't nobody let me roam around like that when I get senile. It's a shame."

"What they going to do about Della? Don't she have no people?"

"A sister's coming up from North Carolina to look after her. I expect she wants to get aholt of Della's house."

"Oh, come on. That's a evil thought, if ever I heard one."

"What you want to bet? Henry Washington said that sister ain't seen Della in fifteen years."

"I kind of thought Henry would marry her one of these days."

"That old woman?"

"Well, Henry ain't no chicken."

"No, but he ain't no buzzard, either."

"He ever been married to anybody?"

"No."

"How come? Somebody cut it off?"

"He's just picky."

"He ain't picky. You see anything around here you'd marry?"

"Well . . . no."

"He's just sensible. A steady worker with quiet ways. I hope it works out all right."

"It will. How much you charging?"
"Five dollars every two weeks."
"That'll be a big help to you."
"I'll say."

Their conversation is like a gently wicked dance: sound meets sound, curtsies, shimmies, and retires. Another sound enters but is upstaged by still another: the two circle each other and stop. Sometimes their words move in lofty spirals; other times they take strident leaps, and all of it is punctuated with warm-pulsed laughter—like the throb of a heart made of jelly. The edge, the curl, the thrust of their emotions is always clear to Frieda and me. We do not, cannot, know the meanings of all their words, for we are nine and ten years old. So we watch their faces, their hands, their feet, and listen for truth in timbre.

So when Mr. Henry arrived on a Saturday night, we smelled him. He smelled wonderful. Like trees and lemon vanishing cream, and Nu Nile Hair Oil and flecks of Sen-Sen.

He smiled a lot, showing small even teeth with a friendly gap in the middle. Frieda and I were not introduced to him—merely pointed out. Like, here is the bathroom; the clothes closet is here; and these are my kids, Frieda and Claudia; watch out for this window; it don't open all the way.

We looked sideways at him, saying nothing and expecting him to say nothing. Just to nod, as he had done at the clothes closet, acknowledging our existence. To our surprise, he spoke to us.

"Hello there. You must be Greta Garbo, and you must be Ginger Rogers."

We giggled. Even my father was startled into a smile.

"Want a penny?" He held out a shiny coin to us. Frieda lowered her head, too pleased to answer. I reached for it. He snapped his thumb and forefinger, and the penny disappeared. Our shock was laced with delight. We searched all over him, poking our fingers into his socks, looking up the inside back of his coat. If happiness is anticipation with certainty, we were happy. And while we waited for the coin to reappear, we knew we were amusing Mama and Daddy. Daddy was smiling, and Mama's eyes went soft as they followed our hands wandering over Mr. Henry's body.

We loved him. Even after what came later, there was no bitterness in our memory of him.

She slept in the bed with us. Frieda on the outside because she is brave—it never occurs to her that if in her sleep her hand hangs over the edge of the bed "something" will crawl out from under it and bite her fingers off. I sleep near the wall because that thought *has* occurred to me. Pecola, therefore, had to sleep in the middle.

Mama had told us two days earlier that a "case" was coming—a girl who had no place to go. The county had placed her in our house for a few days until they could decide what to do, or, more precisely, until the family was reunited. We were to be nice to her and not fight. Mama didn't know "what got into people," but that old

Dog Breedlove had burned up his house, gone upside his wife's head, and everybody, as a result, was outdoors.

Outdoors, we knew, was the real terror of life. The threat of being outdoors surfaced frequently in those days. Every possibility of excess was curtailed with it. If somebody ate too much, he could end up outdoors. If somebody used too much coal, he could end up outdoors. People could gamble themselves outdoors, drink themselves outdoors. Sometimes mothers put their sons outdoors, and when that happened, regardless of what the son had done, all sympathy was with him. He was outdoors, and his own flesh had done it. To be put outdoors by a landlord was one thing—unfortunate, but an aspect of life over which you had no control, since you could not control your income. But to be slack enough to put oneself outdoors, or heartless enough to put one's own kin outdoors—that was criminal.

There is a difference between being put *out* and being put out*doors*. If you are put out, you go somewhere else; if you are outdoors, there is no place to go. The distinction was subtle but final. Outdoors was the end of something, an irrevocable, physical fact, defining and complementing our metaphysical condition. Being a minority in both caste and class, we moved about anyway on the hem of life, struggling to consolidate our weaknesses and hang on, or to creep singly up into the major folds of the garment. Our peripheral existence, however, was something we had learned to deal with—probably because it was abstract. But the concreteness of being outdoors was another matter—like the difference between the concept of death and being, in fact, dead. Dead doesn't change, and outdoors is here to stay.

Knowing that there was such a thing as outdoors bred in us a hunger for property, for ownership. The firm possession of a yard, a porch, a grape arbor. Propertied black people spent all their energies, all their love, on their nests. Like frenzied, desperate birds, they overdecorated everything; fussed and fidgeted over their hard-won homes; canned, jellied, and preserved all summer to fill the cupboards and shelves; they painted, picked, and poked at every corner of their houses. And these houses loomed like hothouse sunflowers among the rows of weeds that were the rented houses. Renting blacks cast furtive glances at these owned yards and porches, and made firmer commitments to buy themselves "some nice little old place." In the meantime, they saved, and scratched, and piled away what they could in the rented hovels, looking forward to the day of property.

Cholly Breedlove, then, a renting black, having put his family outdoors, had catapulted himself beyond the reaches of human consideration. He had joined the animals; was, indeed, an old dog, a snake, a ratty nigger. Mrs. Breedlove was staying with the woman she worked for; the boy, Sammy, was with some other family; and Pecola was to stay with us. Cholly was in jail.

She came with nothing. No little paper bag with the other dress, or a nightgown, or two pair of whitish cotton bloomers. She just appeared with a white woman and sat down.

We had fun in those few days Pecola was with us. Frieda and I stopped fighting each other and concentrated on our guest, trying hard to keep her from feeling outdoors.

When we discovered that she clearly did not want to dominate us, we liked her. She laughed when I clowned for her, and smiled and accepted gracefully the food gifts my sister gave her.

"Would you like some graham crackers?"

"I don't care."

Frieda brought her four graham crackers on a saucer and some milk in a blue-and-white Shirley Temple cup. She was a long time with the milk, and gazed fondly at the silhouette of Shirley Temple's dimpled face. Frieda and she had a loving conversation about how cu-ute Shirley Temple was. I couldn't join them in their adoration because I hated Shirley. Not because she was cute, but because she danced with Bojangles, who was *my* friend, *my* uncle, *my* daddy, and who ought to have been soft-shoeing it and chuckling with me. Instead he was enjoying, sharing, giving a lovely dance thing with one of those little white girls whose socks never slid down under their heels. So I said, "I like Jane Withers."

They gave me a puzzled look, decided I was incomprehensible, and continued their reminiscing about old squint-eyed Shirley.

Younger than both Frieda and Pecola, I had not yet arrived at the turning point in the development of my psyche which would allow me to love her. What I felt at that time was unsullied hatred. But before that I had felt a stranger, more frightening thing than hatred for all the Shirley Temples of the world.

It had begun with Christmas and the gift of dolls. The

big, the special, the loving gift was always a big,
blue-eyed Baby Doll. From the clucking sounds of adults
I knew that the doll represented what they thought was
my fondest wish. I was bemused with the thing itself, and
the way it looked. What was I supposed to do with it?
Pretend I was its mother? I had no interest in babies or
the concept of motherhood. I was interested only in
humans my own age and size, and could not generate any
enthusiasm at the prospect of being a mother.
Motherhood was old age, and other remote possibilities. I
learned quickly, however, what I was expected to do with
the doll: rock it, fabricate storied situations around it,
even sleep with it. Picture books were full of little girls
sleeping with their dolls. Raggedy Ann dolls usually, but
they were out of the question. I was physically revolted
by and secretly frightened of those round moronic eyes,
the pancake face, and orangeworms hair.

The other dolls, which were supposed to bring me
great pleasure, succeeded in doing quite the opposite.
When I took it to bed, its hard unyielding limbs resisted
my flesh—the tapered fingertips on those dimpled hands
scratched. If, in sleep, I turned, the bone-cold head
collided with my own. It was a most uncomfortable,
patently aggressive sleeping companion. To hold it was
no more rewarding. The starched gauze or lace on the
cotton dress irritated any embrace. I had only one desire:
to dismember it. To see of what it was made, to discover
the dearness, to find the beauty, the desirability that had
escaped me, but apparently only me. Adults, older girls,
shops, magazines, newspapers, window signs—all the
world had agreed that a blue-eyed, yellow-haired,
pink-skinned doll was what every girl child treasured.

"Here," they said, "this is beautiful, and if you are on this day 'worthy' you may have it." I fingered the face, wondering at the single-stroke eyebrows; picked at the pearly teeth stuck like two piano keys between red bowline lips. Traced the turned-up nose, poked the glassy blue eyeballs, twisted the yellow hair. I could not love it. But I could examine it to see what it was that all the world said was lovable. Break off the tiny fingers, bend the flat feet, loosen the hair, twist the head around, and the thing made one sound—a sound they said was the sweet and plaintive cry "Mama," but which sounded to me like the bleat of a dying lamb, or, more precisely, our icebox door opening on rusty hinges in July. Remove the cold and stupid eyeball, it would bleat still, "Ahhhhhh," take off the head, shake out the sawdust, crack the back against the brass bed rail, it would bleat still. The gauze back would split, and I could see the disk with six holes, the secret of the sound. A mere metal roundness.

Grown people frowned and fussed: "You-don't-know-how-to-take-care-of-nothing. I-never-had-a-baby-doll-in-my-whole-life-and-used-to-cry-my-eyes-out-for-them. Now-you-got-one-a-beautiful-one-and-you-tear-it-up-what's-the-matter-with-you?"

How strong was their outrage. Tears threatened to erase the aloofness of their authority. The emotion of years of unfulfilled longing preened in their voices. I did not know why I destroyed those dolls. But I did know that nobody ever asked me what I wanted for Christmas. Had any adult with the power to fulfill my desires taken me seriously and asked me what I wanted, they would have known that I did not want to have anything to own, or to possess any object. I wanted rather to feel something on Christmas day. The real question would have been, "Dear Claudia, what experience would you like on Christmas?" I could have spoken up, "I want to sit on the low stool in Big Mama's kitchen with my lap full of lilacs and listen to Big Papa play his violin for me alone." The lowness of the stool made for my body, the security and warmth of Big Mama's kitchen, the smell of the lilacs, the sound of the music, and, since it would be good to have all of my senses engaged, the taste of a peach, perhaps, afterward.

Instead I tasted and smelled the acridness of tin plates and cups designed for tea parties that bored me. Instead I looked with loathing on new dresses that required a hateful bath in a galvanized zinc tub before wearing. Slipping around on the zinc, no time to play or soak, for the water chilled too fast, no time to enjoy one's nakedness, only time to make curtains of soapy water career down between the legs. Then the scratchy towels and the dreadful and humiliating absence of dirt. The irritable, unimaginative cleanliness. Gone the ink marks from legs and face, all my creations and accumulations of the day gone, and replaced by goose pimples.

I destroyed white baby dolls.

But the dismembering of dolls was not the true horror. The truly horrifying thing was the transference of the same impulses to little white girls. The indifference with which I could have axed them was shaken only by my desire to do so. To discover what eluded me: the secret of the magic they weaved on others. What made people look at them and say, "Awwwww," but not for me? The eye slide of black women as they approached them on the street, and the possessive gentleness of their touch as they handled them.

If I pinched them, their eyes—unlike the crazed glint of the baby doll's eyes—would fold in pain, and their cry would not be the sound of an icebox door, but a fascinating cry of pain. When I learned how repulsive this disinterested violence was, that it was repulsive because it was disinterested, my shame floundered about for refuge. The best hiding place was love. Thus the conversion from pristine sadism to fabricated hatred, to fraudulent love. It was a small step to Shirley Temple. I learned much later to worship her, just as I learned to delight in cleanliness, knowing, even as I learned, that the change was adjustment without improvement.

"Three quarts of milk. That's what was *in* that icebox yesterday. Three whole quarts. Now they ain't none. Not a drop. I don't mind folks coming in and getting what they want, but three quarts of milk! What the devil does *any*body need with *three* quarts of milk?"

The "folks" my mother was referring to was Pecola. The three of us, Pecola, Frieda, and I, listened to her downstairs in the kitchen fussing about the amount of milk Pecola had drunk. We knew she was fond of the Shirley Temple cup and took every opportunity to drink milk out of it just to handle and see sweet Shirley's face. My mother knew that Frieda and I hated milk and assumed Pecola drank it out of greediness. It was certainly not for us to "dispute" her. We didn't initiate talk with grown-ups; we answered their questions.

Ashamed of the insults that were being heaped on our
friend, we just sat there: I picked toe jam, Frieda cleaned
her fingernails with her teeth, and Pecola finger-traced
some scars on her knee—her head cocked to one side.
My mother's fussing soliloquies always irritated and
depressed us. They were interminable, insulting, and
although indirect (Mama never named anybody—just
talked about folks and *some* people), extremely painful in
their thrust. She would go on like that for hours,
connecting one offense to another until all of the things
that chagrined her were spewed out. Then, having told
everybody and everything off, she would burst into song
and sing the rest of the day. But it was such a long time
before the singing part came. In the meantime, our
stomachs jellying and our necks burning, we listened,
avoided each other's eyes, and picked toe jam or
whatever.

". . . I don't know what I'm suppose to be running
here, a charity ward, I guess. Time for me to get out of
the *giving* line and get in the *getting* line. I guess I ain't
sup*posed* to have nothing. I'm sup*posed* to end up in the
poorhouse. Look like nothing I do is going to keep me
out of there. Folks just spend all their time trying to
figure out ways to send *me* to the poorhouse. I got about
as much business with another mouth to feed as a cat has
with side pockets. As if I don't have trouble enough
trying to feed my own and keep out the poorhouse, now
I got something else in here that's just going to *drink* me
on in there. Well, naw, she ain't. Not long as I got
strength in my body and a tongue in my head. There's a
limit to everything. I ain't got nothing to just throw
away. Don't *nobody* need *three* quarts of milk. Henry

Ford don't need three quarts of milk. That's just downright *sin*ful. I'm willing to do what I can for folks. Can't nobody say I ain't. But this has got to stop, and I'm just the one to stop it. Bible say watch as *well* as pray. Folks just dump they children off on you and go on 'bout they business. Ain't nobody even *peeped* in here to see whether that child has a loaf of bread. Look like they would just *peep* in to see whether I had a loaf of bread to give her. But naw. That thought don't cross they mind. That old trifling Cholly been out of jail *two* whole days and ain't been here *yet* to see if his own child was 'live or dead. She could be *dead* for all he know. And that *mama* neither. What kind of something is that?"

When Mama got around to Henry Ford and all those people who didn't care whether she had a loaf of bread, it was time to go. We wanted to miss the part about Roosevelt and the CCC camps.

Frieda got up and started down the stairs. Pecola and I followed, making a wide arc to avoid the kitchen doorway. We sat on the steps of the porch, where my mother's words could reach us only in spurts.

It was a lonesome Saturday. The house smelled of Fels Naphtha and the sharp odor of mustard greens cooking. Saturdays were lonesome, fussy, soapy days. Second in misery only to those tight, starchy, cough-drop Sundays, so full of "don'ts" and "set'cha self downs."

If my mother was in a singing mood, it wasn't so bad. She would sing about hard times, bad times, and somebody-done-gone-and-left-me times. But her voice was so sweet and her singing-eyes so melty I found myself longing for those hard times, yearning to be grown without "a thin di-i-ime to my name." I looked forward to the delicious time when "my man" would leave me, when I would "hate to see that evening sun go down . . ." 'cause then I would know "my man has left this town." Misery colored by the greens and blues in my mother's voice took all of the grief out of the words and left me with a conviction that pain was not only endurable, it was sweet.

But without song, those Saturdays sat on my head like a coal scuttle, and if Mama was fussing, as she was now, it was like somebody throwing stones at it.

". . . and here I am poor as a bowl of yak-me. What do they think I am? Some kind of Sandy Claus? Well, they can just take they stocking down 'cause it *ain't* Christmas. . . ."

We fidgeted.

"Let's do something," Frieda said.

"What do you want to do?" I asked.

"I don't know. Nothing." Frieda stared at the tops of the trees. Pecola looked at her feet.

"You want to go up to Mr. Henry's room and look at his girlie magazines?"

Frieda made an ugly face. She didn't like to look at dirty pictures. "Well," I continued, "we could look at his Bible. *That's* pretty." Frieda sucked her teeth and made a *phttt* sound with her lips. "O.K., then. We could go thread needles for the half-blind lady. She'll give us a penny."

Frieda snorted. "Her eyes look like snot. I don't feel like looking at them. What *you* want to do, Pecola?"

"I don't care," she said. "Anything you want."

I had another idea. "We could go up the alley and see what's in the trash cans."

"Too cold," said Frieda. She was bored and irritable.

"I know. We could make some fudge."

"You kidding? With Mama in there fussing? When she starts fussing at the walls, you know she's gonna be at it all day. She wouldn't even let us."

"Well, let's go over to the Greek hotel and listen to them cuss."

"Oh, who wants to do *that*? Besides, they say the same old words all the time."

My supply of ideas exhausted, I began to concentrate on the white spots on my fingernails. The total signified the number of boyfriends I would have. Seven.

Mama's soliloquy slid into the silence ". . . Bible say feed the hungry. That's fine. That's all right. But I ain't feeding no elephants. . . . Anybody need three quarts of milk to *live* need to get out of here. They in the wrong place. What is this? Some kind of *dairy* farm?"

Suddenly Pecola bolted straight up, her eyes wide with terror. A whinnying sound came from her mouth.

"What's the matter with *you*?" Frieda stood up too.

Then we both looked where Pecola was staring. Blood was running down her legs. Some drops were on the steps. I leaped up. "Hey. You cut yourself? Look. It's all over your dress."

A brownish-red stain discolored the back of her dress. She kept whinnying, standing with her legs far apart.

Frieda said, "Oh. Lordy! I know. I know what that is!"

"What?" Pecola's fingers went to her mouth.

"That's ministratin'."

"What's that?"

"You know."

"Am I going to die?" she asked.

"Noooo. You won't die. It just means you can have a baby!"

"What?"

"How do *you* know?" I was sick and tired of Frieda knowing everything.

"Mildred told me, and Mama too."

"I don't believe it."

"You don't have to, dummy. Look. Wait here. Sit down, Pecola. Right here." Frieda was all authority and zest. "And you," she said to me, "you go get some water."

"Water?"

"Yes, stupid. Water. And be quiet, or Mama will hear you."

Pecola sat down again, a little less fear in her eyes. I went into the kitchen.

"What you want, girl?" Mama was rinsing curtains in the sink.

"Some water, ma'am."

"Right where I'm working, naturally. Well, get a glass. Not no clean one neither. Use that jar."

I got a Mason jar and filled it with water from the faucet. It seemed a long time filling.

"Don't nobody never want nothing till they see me at the sink. Then everybody got to drink water. . . ."

When the jar was full, I moved to leave the room.

"Where you going?"

"Outside."

"Drink that water right here!"

"I ain't gonna break nothing."

"You don't know what you gonna do."

"Yes, ma'am. I do. Lemme take it out. I won't spill none."

"You bed' not."

I got to the porch and stood there with the Mason jar of water. Pecola was crying.

"What you crying for? Does it hurt?"

She shook her head.

"Then stop slinging snot."

Frieda opened the back door. She had something tucked in her blouse. She looked at me in amazement and pointed to the jar. "What's that supposed to do?"

"You told me. You *said* get some water."

"Not a little old jar full. Lots of water. To scrub the steps with, dumbbell!"

"How was I supposed to know?"

"Yeah: How was you. Come on." She pulled Pecola up by the arm. "Let's go back here." They headed for the side of the house where the bushes were thick.

"Hey. What about me? I want to go."

"Shut uuuup," Frieda stage-whispered. "Mama will hear you. You wash the steps."

They disappeared around the corner of the house.

I was going to miss something. Again. Here was something important, and I had to stay behind and not see any of it. I poured the water on the steps, sloshed it with my shoe, and ran to join them.

Frieda was on her knees; a white rectangle of cotton was near her on the ground. She was pulling Pecola's pants off. "Come on. Step out of them." She managed to get the soiled pants down and flung them at me. "Here."

"What am I supposed to do with these?"

"Bury them, moron."

Frieda told Pecola to hold the cotton thing between her legs.

"How she gonna walk like that?" I asked.

Frieda didn't answer. Instead she took two safety pins from the hem of her skirt and began to pin the ends of the napkin to Pecola's dress.

I picked up the pants with two fingers and looked about for something to dig a hole with. A rustling noise in the bushes startled me, and turning toward it, I saw a pair of fascinated eyes in a dough-white face. Rosemary was watching us. I grabbed for her face and succeeded in scratching her nose. She screamed and jumped back.

"Mrs. MacTeer! Mrs. MacTeer!" Rosemary hollered. "Frieda and Claudia are out here playing nasty! Mrs. MacTeer!"

Mama opened the window and looked down at us.

"What?"

"They're playing nasty, Mrs. MacTeer. Look. And Claudia hit me 'cause I seen them!"

Mama slammed the window shut and came running out the back door.

"What you all doing? Oh. Uh-huh. Uh-huh. Playing nasty, huh?" She reached into the bushes and pulled off a switch. "I'd rather raise pigs than some nasty girls. Least I can slaughter *them!*"

We began to shriek. "No, Mama. No, ma'am. We wasn't! She's a liar! No, ma'am, Mama! No, ma'am, Mama!"

Mama grabbed Frieda by the shoulder, turned her around, and gave her three or four stinging cuts on her legs. "Gonna be nasty, huh? Naw you ain't!"

Frieda was destroyed. Whippings wounded and insulted her.

Mama looked at Pecola. "You too!" she said. "Child of mine or not!" She grabbed Pecola and spun her around. The safety pin snapped open on one end of the napkin, and Mama saw it fall from under her dress. The switch hovered in the air while Mama blinked. "What the devil is going on here?"

Frieda was sobbing. I, next in line, began to explain. "She was bleeding. We was just trying to stop the blood!"

Mama looked at Frieda for verification. Frieda nodded. "She's ministratin'. We was just helping."

Mama released Pecola and stood looking at her. Then she pulled both of them toward her, their heads against her stomach. Her eyes were sorry. "All right, all right. Now, stop crying. I didn't know. Come on, now. Get on in the house. Go on home, Rosemary. The show is over."

We trooped in, Frieda sobbing quietly, Pecola carrying a white tail, me carrying the little-girl-gone-to-woman pants.

Mama led us to the bathroom. She prodded Pecola inside, and taking the underwear from me, told us to stay out.

We could hear water running into the bathtub.

"You think she's going to drown her?"

"Oh, Claudia. You so dumb. She's just going to wash her clothes and all."

"Should we beat up Rosemary?"

"No. Leave her alone."

The water gushed, and over its gushing we could hear the music of my mother's laughter.

That night, in bed, the three of us lay still. We were full of awe and respect for Pecola. Lying next to a real person who was really ministratin' was somehow sacred. She was different from us now—grown-up-like. She, herself, felt the distance, but refused to lord it over us.

After a long while she spoke very softly. "Is it true that I can have a baby now?"

"Sure," said Frieda drowsily. "Sure you can."

"But . . . how?" Her voice was hollow with wonder.

"Oh," said Frieda, "somebody has to love you."

"Oh."

There was a long pause in which Pecola and I thought this over. It would involve, I supposed, "my man," who, before leaving me, would love me. But there weren't any babies in the songs my mother sang. Maybe that's why the women were sad: the men left before they could make a baby.

Then Pecola asked a question that had never entered my mind. "How do you do that? I mean, how do you get somebody to love you?" But Frieda was asleep. And I didn't know.

HEREISTHEHOUSEITISGREENANDWH
ITEITHASAREDDOORITISVERYPRETT
YITISVERYPRETTYPRETTYPRETTYP

There is an abandoned store on the southeast corner of Broadway and Thirty-fifth Street in Lorain, Ohio. It does not recede into its background of leaden sky, nor harmonize with the gray frame houses and black telephone poles around it. Rather, it foists itself on the eye of the passerby in a manner that is both irritating and melancholy. Visitors who drive to this tiny town wonder why it has not been torn down, while pedestrians, who are residents of the neighborhood, simply look away when they pass it.

At one time, when the building housed a pizza parlor, people saw only slow-footed teen-aged boys huddled about the corner. These young boys met there to feel their groins, smoke cigarettes, and plan mild outrages. The smoke from their cigarettes they inhaled deeply, forcing it to fill their lungs, their hearts, their thighs, and keep at bay the shiveriness, the energy of their youth. They moved slowly, laughed slowly, but flicked the ashes from their cigarettes too quickly too often, and exposed themselves, to those who were interested, as novices to the habit. But long before the sound of their lowing and the sight of their preening, the building was leased to a Hungarian baker, modestly famous for his brioche and poppy-seed rolls. Earlier than that, there was a real-estate office there, and even before that, some gypsies used it as a base of operations. The gypsy family gave the large plate-glass window as much distinction and character as it ever had. The girls of the family took turns sitting between yards of velvet draperies and Oriental rugs hanging at the windows. They looked out and occasionally smiled, or winked, or beckoned—only occasionally. Mostly they looked, their elaborate dresses, long-sleeved and long-skirted, hiding the nakedness that stood in their eyes.

So fluid has the population in that area been, that probably no one remembers longer, longer ago, before the time of the gypsies and the time of the teen-agers when the Breedloves lived there, nestled together in the storefront. Festering together in the debris of a realtor's whim. They slipped in and out of the box of peeling gray, making no stir in the neighborhood, no sound in the labor force, and no wave in the mayor's office. Each member of the family in his own cell of consciousness, each making his own patchwork quilt of reality—collecting fragments of experience here, pieces of information there. From the tiny impressions gleaned from one another, they created a sense of belonging and tried to make do with the way they found each other.

The plan of the living quarters was as unimaginative as a first-generation Greek landlord could contrive it to be. The large "store" area was partitioned into two rooms by beaverboard planks that did not reach to the ceiling. There was a living room, which the family called the front room, and the bedroom, where all the living was done. In the front room were two sofas, an upright piano, and a tiny artificial Christmas tree which had been there, decorated and dust-laden, for two years. The bedroom had three beds: a narrow iron bed for Sammy, fourteen years old, another for Pecola, eleven years old, and a double bed for Cholly and Mrs. Breedlove. In the center of the bedroom, for the even distribution of heat, stood a coal stove. Trunks, chairs, a small end table, and a cardboard "wardrobe" closet were placed around the walls. The kitchen was in the back of this apartment, a separate room. There were no bath facilities. Only a toilet bowl, inaccessible to the eye, if not the ear, of the tenants.

There is nothing more to say about the furnishings. They were anything but describable, having been conceived, manufactured, shipped, and sold in various states of thoughtlessness, greed, and indifference. The furniture had aged without ever having become familiar. People had owned it, but never known it. No one had lost a penny or a brooch under the cushions of either sofa and remembered the place and time of the loss or the finding. No one had clucked and said, "But I *had* it just a minute ago. I was sitting right there talking to . . ." or "Here it is. It must have slipped down while I was feeding the baby!" No one had given birth in one of the beds—or remembered with fondness the peeled paint places, because that's what the baby, when he learned to pull himself up, used to pick loose. No thrifty child had tucked a wad of gum under the table. No happy drunk—a friend of the family, with a fat neck, unmarried, you know, but God how he eats!—had sat at the piano and played "You Are My Sunshine." No young girl had stared at the

tiny Christmas tree and remembered when she had decorated it, or wondered if that blue ball was going to hold, or
if HE would ever come back to see it.

There were no memories among those pieces. Certainly
no memories to be cherished. Occasionally an item provoked a physical reaction: an increase of acid irritation in
the upper intestinal tract, a light flush of perspiration at the
back of the neck as circumstances surrounding the piece of
furniture were recalled. The sofa, for example. It had been
purchased new, but the fabric had split straight across the
back by the time it was delivered. The store would not take
the responsibility. . . .

"Looka here, buddy. It was O.K. when I put it on the
truck. The store can't do anything about it once it's on the
truck. . . ." Listerine and Lucky Strike breath.

"But I don't want no tore couch if'n it's bought new."
Pleading eyes and tightened testicles.

"Tough shit, buddy. *Your* tough shit. . . ."

You could hate a sofa, of course—that is, if you could
hate a sofa. But it didn't matter. You still had to get together
$4.80 a month. If you had to pay $4.80 a month for a sofa
that started off split, no good, and humiliating—you
couldn't take any joy in owning it. And the joylessness
stank, pervading everything. The stink of it kept you from
painting the beaverboard walls; from getting a matching
piece of material for the chair; even from sewing up the split,
which became a gash, which became a gaping chasm that
exposed the cheap frame and cheaper upholstery. It withheld the refreshment in a sleep slept on it. It imposed a
furtiveness on the loving done on it. Like a sore tooth that
is not content to throb in isolation, but must diffuse its own
pain to other parts of the body—making breathing difficult,

vision limited, nerves unsettled, so a hated piece of furniture produces a fretful malaise that asserts itself throughout the house and limits the delight of things not related to it.

The only living thing in the Breedloves' house was the coal stove, which lived independently of everything and everyone, its fire being "out," "banked," or "up" at its own discretion, in spite of the fact that the family fed it and knew all the details of its regimen: sprinkle, do not dump, not too much. . . . The fire seemed to live, go down, or die according to its own schemata. In the morning, however, it always saw fit to die.

HEREISTHEFAMILYMOTHERFATHER
DICKANDJANETHEYLIVEINTHEGREE
NANDWHITEHOUSETHEYAREVERYH

The Breedloves did not live in a storefront because they were having temporary difficulty adjusting to the cutbacks at the plant. They lived there because they were poor and black, and they stayed there because they believed they were ugly. Although their poverty was traditional and stultifying, it was not unique. But their ugliness was unique. No one could have convinced them that they were not relentlessly and aggressively ugly. Except for the father, Cholly, whose ugliness (the result of despair, dissipation, and violence directed toward petty things and weak people) was behavior, the rest of the family—Mrs. Breedlove, Sammy Breedlove, and Pecola Breedlove—wore their ugliness, put it on, so to speak, although it did not belong to them. The eyes, the small eyes set closely together under narrow foreheads. The low, irregular hairlines, which seemed even more irregular in contrast to the straight, heavy eyebrows which nearly met. Keen but crooked noses, with insolent nostrils. They had high cheekbones, and their ears turned forward.

Shapely lips which called attention not to themselves but to the rest of the face. You looked at them and wondered why they were so ugly; you looked closely and could not find the source. Then you realized that it came from conviction, their conviction. It was as though some mysterious all-knowing master had given each one a cloak of ugliness to wear, and they had each accepted it without question. The master had said, "You are ugly people." They had looked about themselves and saw nothing to contradict the statement; saw, in fact, support for it leaning at them from every billboard, every movie, every glance. "Yes," they had said. "You are right." And they took the ugliness in their hands, threw it as a mantle over them, and went about the world with it. Dealing with it each according to his way. Mrs. Breedlove handled hers as an actor does a prop: for the articulation of character, for support of a role she frequently imagined was hers—martyrdom. Sammy used his as a weapon to cause others pain. He adjusted his behavior to it, chose his companions on the basis of it: people who could be fascinated, even intimidated by it. And Pecola. She hid behind hers. Concealed, veiled, eclipsed—peeping out from behind the shroud very seldom, and then only to yearn for the return of her mask.

This family, on a Saturday morning in October, began, one by one, to stir out of their dreams of affluence and vengeance into the anonymous misery of their storefront.

Mrs. Breedlove slipped noiselessly out of bed, put a sweater on over her nightgown (which was an old day dress), and walked toward the kitchen. Her one good foot made hard, bony sounds; the twisted one whispered on the linoleum. In the kitchen she made noises with doors, faucets, and pans. The noises were hollow, but the threats they implied were not. Pecola opened her eyes and lay staring at the dead coal stove. Cholly mumbled, thrashed about in the bed for a minute, and then was quiet.

Even from where Pecola lay, she could smell Cholly's whiskey. The noises in the kitchen became louder and less hollow. There was direction and purpose in Mrs. Breedlove's movements that had nothing to do with the preparation of breakfast. This awareness, supported by ample evidence from the past, made Pecola tighten her stomach muscles and ration her breath.

Cholly had come home drunk. Unfortunately he had been too drunk to quarrel, so the whole business would have to erupt this morning. Because it had not taken place immediately, the oncoming fight would lack spontaneity; it would be calculated, uninspired, and deadly.

Mrs. Breedlove came swiftly into the room and stood at the foot of the bed where Cholly lay.

"I need some coal in this house."

Cholly did not move.

"Hear me?" Mrs. Breedlove jabbed Cholly's foot.

Cholly opened his eyes slowly. They were red and menacing. With no exception, Cholly had the meanest eyes in town.

"Awwwwww, woman!"

"I said I need some coal. It's as cold as a witch's tit in this house. Your whiskey ass wouldn't feel hellfire, but I'm cold. I got to do a lot of things, but I ain't got to freeze."

"Leave me 'lone."

"Not until you get me some coal. If working like a mule don't give me the right to be warm, what am I doing it for?

You sure ain't bringing in nothing. If it was left up to you, we'd all be dead. . . ." Her voice was like an earache in the brain. ". . . If you think I'm going to wade out in the cold and get it myself, you'd better think again."

"I don't give a shit how you get it." A bubble of violence burst in his throat.

"You going to get your drunk self out of that bed and get me some coal or not?"

Silence.

"Cholly!"

Silence.

"Don't try me this morning, man. You say one more word, and I'll split you open!"

Silence.

"All right. All right. But if I sneeze once, just once, God help your butt!"

Sammy was awake now too, but pretending to be asleep. Pecola still held her stomach muscles taut and conserved her breath. They all knew that Mrs. Breedlove could have, would have, and had, gotten coal from the shed, or that Sammy or Pecola could be directed to get it. But the unquarreled evening hung like the first note of a dirge in sullenly expectant air. An escapade of drunkenness, no matter how routine, had its own ceremonial close. The tiny, undistinguished days that Mrs. Breedlove lived were identified, grouped, and classed by these quarrels. They gave substance to the minutes and hours otherwise dim and unrecalled. They relieved the tiresomeness of poverty, gave grandeur to the dead rooms. In these violent breaks in routine that were themselves routine, she could display the style and imagination of what she believed to be her own true self. To deprive her of these fights was to deprive her of all the zest and reasonableness of life. Cholly, by his habitual drunkenness and orneriness, provided them both with the material they needed to make their lives tolerable. Mrs. Breedlove considered herself an upright and Christian woman, burdened with a no-count man, whom God wanted her to punish. (Cholly was beyond redemption, of course, and redemption was hardly the point—Mrs. Breedlove was not interested in Christ the Redeemer, but rather Christ the Judge.) Often she could be heard discoursing with Jesus about Cholly, pleading with Him to help her "strike the bastard down from his pea-knuckle of pride." And once when a drunken gesture catapulted Cholly into the red-hot stove, she screamed, "Get him, Jesus! Get him!" If Cholly had stopped drinking, she would never have forgiven Jesus. She needed Cholly's sins desperately. The lower he sank, the wilder and more irresponsible he became, the more splendid she and her task became. In the name of Jesus.

No less did Cholly need her. She was one of the few things abhorrent to him that he could touch and therefore hurt. He poured out on her the sum of all his inarticulate fury and aborted desires. Hating her, he could leave himself intact. When he was still very young, Cholly had been surprised in some bushes by two white men while he was newly but earnestly engaged in eliciting sexual pleasure from a little country girl. The men had shone a flashlight right on his behind. He had stopped, terrified. They chuckled. The beam of the flashlight did not move. "Go on," they said. "Go on and finish. And, nigger, make it good." The flashlight did not move. For some reason Cholly had not hated the white men; he hated, despised, the girl. Even a half-remembrance of this episode, along with myriad other humiliations, defeats, and emasculations, could stir him into flights of depravity that surprised himself—but only himself. Somehow he could not astound. He could only be astounded. So he gave that up, too.

Cholly and Mrs. Breedlove fought each other with a darkly brutal formalism that was paralleled only by their lovemaking. Tacitly they had agreed not to kill each other. He fought her the way a coward fights a man—with feet, the palms of his hands, and teeth. She, in turn, fought back in a purely feminine way—with frying pans and pokers, and occasionally a flatiron would sail toward his head. They did not talk, groan, or curse during these beatings. There was only the muted sound of falling things, and flesh on unsurprised flesh.

There was a difference in the reaction of the children to these battles. Sammy cursed for a while, or left the house, or threw himself into the fray. He was known, by the time he was fourteen, to have run away from home no less than twenty-seven times. Once he got to Buffalo and stayed three months. His returns, whether by force or circumstance, were sullen. Pecola, on the other hand, restricted by youth and sex, experimented with methods of endurance. Though the methods varied, the pain was as consistent as it was deep. She struggled between an overwhelming desire that one would kill the other, and a profound wish that she herself could die. Now she was whispering, "Don't, Mrs. Breedlove. Don't." Pecola, like Sammy and Cholly, always called her mother Mrs. Breedlove.

"Don't, Mrs. Breedlove. Don't."

But Mrs. Breedlove did.

By the grace, no doubt, of God, Mrs. Breedlove sneezed. Just once.

She ran into the bedroom with a dishpan full of cold

water and threw it in Cholly's face. He sat up, choking and spitting. Naked and ashen, he leaped from the bed, and with a flying tackle, grabbed his wife around the waist, and they hit the floor. Cholly picked her up and knocked her down with the back of his hand. She fell in a sitting position, her back supported by Sammy's bed frame. She had not let go of the dishpan, and began to hit at Cholly's thighs and groin with it. He put his foot in her chest, and she dropped the pan. Dropping to his knee, he struck her several times in the face, and she might have succumbed early had he not hit his hand against the metal bed frame when his wife ducked. Mrs. Breedlove took advantage of this momentary suspension of blows and slipped out of his reach. Sammy, who had watched in silence their struggling at his bedside, suddenly began to hit his father about the head with both fists, shouting "You naked fuck!" over and over and over. Mrs. Breedlove, having snatched up the round, flat stove lid, ran tippy-toe to Cholly as he was pulling himself up from his knees, and struck him two blows, knocking him right back into the senselessness out of which she had provoked him. Panting, she threw a quilt over him and let him lie.

Sammy screamed, "Kill him! Kill him!"

Mrs. Breedlove looked at Sammy with surprise. "Cut out that noise, boy." She put the stove lid back in place, and walked toward the kitchen. At the doorway she paused long enough to say to her son, "Get up from there anyhow. I need some coal."

Letting herself breathe easy now, Pecola covered her head with the quilt. The sick feeling, which she had tried to prevent by holding in her stomach, came quickly in spite of her precaution. There surged in her the desire to heave, but as always, she knew she would not.

"Please, God," she whispered into the palm of her hand. "Please make me disappear." She squeezed her eyes shut. Little parts of her body faded away. Now slowly, now with a rush. Slowly again. Her fingers went, one by one; then her arms disappeared all the way to the elbow. Her feet now. Yes, that was good. The legs all at once. It was hardest above the thighs. She had to be real still and pull. Her stomach would not go. But finally it, too, went away. Then her chest, her neck. The face was hard, too. Almost done, almost. Only her tight, tight eyes were left. They were always left.

Try as she might, she could never get her eyes to disappear. So what was the point? They were everything. Everything was there, in them. All of those pictures, all of those faces. She had long ago given up the idea of running away to see new pictures, new faces, as Sammy had so often done. He never took her, and he never thought about his going ahead of time, so it was never planned. It wouldn't have worked anyway. As long as she looked the way she did, as long as she was ugly, she would have to stay with these people. Somehow she belonged to them. Long hours she sat looking in the mirror, trying to discover the secret of the ugliness, the ugliness that made her ignored or despised at school, by teachers and classmates alike. She was the only member of her class who sat alone at a double desk. The first letter of her last name forced her to sit in the front of the room always. But what about Marie Appolonaire? Marie was in front of her, but she shared a desk with Luke Angelino. Her teachers had always treated her this way. They tried never to glance at her, and called on her only when everyone was required to respond. She also knew that when one of the girls at school wanted to be particularly insulting to a boy, or wanted to get an immediate response from him, she could say. "Bobby loves Pecola Breedlove! Bobby loves Pecola Breedlove!" and never fail to get peals of laughter from those in earshot, and mock anger from the accused.

It had occurred to Pecola some time ago that if her eyes, those eyes that held the pictures, and knew the sights—if those eyes of hers were different, that is to say, beautiful, she herself would be different. Her teeth were good, and at least her nose was not big and flat like some of those who were thought so cute. If she looked different, beautiful, maybe Cholly would be different, and Mrs. Breedlove too. Maybe they'd say, "Why, look at pretty-eyed Pecola. We mustn't do bad things in front of those pretty eyes."

Pretty eyes. Pretty blue eyes. Big blue pretty eyes.
Run, Jip, run. Jip runs, Alice runs. Alice has blue eyes.
Jerry has blue eyes. Jerry runs. Alice runs. They run
with their blue eyes. Four blue eyes. Four pretty
blue eyes. Blue-sky eyes. Blue-like Mrs. Forrest's
blue blouse eyes. Morning-glory-blue-eyes.
Alice-and-Jerry-blue-storybook-eyes.

Each night, without fail, she prayed for blue eyes. Fervently, for a year she had prayed. Although somewhat discouraged, she was not without hope. To have something as wonderful as that happen would take a long, long time.

Thrown, in this way, into the binding conviction that only a miracle could relieve her, she would never know her beauty. She would see only what there was to see: the eyes of other people.

She walks down Garden Avenue to a small grocery store which sells penny candy. Three pennies are in her shoe— slipping back and forth between the sock and the inner sole. With each step she feels the painful press of the coins against her foot. A sweet, endurable, even cherished irritation, full of promise and delicate security. There is plenty of time to consider what to buy. Now, however, she moves down an avenue gently buffeted by the familiar and therefore loved images. The dandelions at the base of the telephone pole. Why, she wonders, do people call them weeds? She thought they were pretty. But grown-ups say, "Miss Dunion keeps her yard so nice. Not a dandelion anywhere." Hunkie women in black babushkas go into the fields with baskets to pull them up. But they do not want the yellow heads—only the jagged leaves. They make dandelion soup. Dandelion wine. Nobody loves the head of a dandelion. Maybe because they are so many, strong, and soon.

There was the sidewalk crack shaped like a Y, and the other one that lifted the concrete up from the dirt floor. Frequently her sloughing step had made her trip over that one. Skates would go well over this sidewalk—old it was, and smooth; it made the wheels glide evenly, with a mild whirr. The newly paved walks were bumpy and uncomfortable, and the sound of skate wheels on new walks was grating.

These and other inanimate things she saw and experienced. They were real to her. She knew them. They were the codes and touchstones of the world, capable of translation and possession. She owned the crack that made her stumble;

she owned the clumps of dandelions whose white heads, last fall, she had blown away; whose yellow heads, this fall, she peered into. And owning them made her part of the world, and the world a part of her.

She climbs four wooden steps to the door of Yacobowski's Fresh Veg. Meat and Sundries Store. A bell tinkles as she opens it. Standing before the counter, she looks at the array of candies. All Mary Janes, she decides. Three for a penny. The resistant sweetness that breaks open at last to deliver peanut butter—the oil and salt which complement the sweet pull of caramel. A peal of anticipation unsettles her stomach.

She pulls off her shoe and takes out the three pennies. The gray head of Mr. Yacobowski looms up over the counter. He urges his eyes out of his thoughts to encounter her. Blue eyes. Blear-dropped. Slowly, like Indian summer moving imperceptibly toward fall, he looks toward her. Somewhere between retina and object, between vision and view, his eyes draw back, hesitate, and hover. At some fixed point in time and space he senses that he need not waste the effort of a glance. He does not see her, because for him there is nothing to see. How can a fifty-two-year-old white immigrant store-keeper with the taste of potatoes and beer in his mouth, his mind honed on the doe-eyed Virgin Mary, his sensibilities blunted by a permanent awareness of loss, *see* a little black girl? Nothing in his life even suggested that the feat was possible, not to say desirable or necessary.

"Yeah?"

She looks up at him and sees the vacuum where curiosity ought to lodge. And something more. The total absence of human recognition—the glazed separateness. She does not know what keeps his glance suspended. Perhaps because he is grown, or a man, and she a little girl. But she has seen interest, disgust, even anger in grown male eyes. Yet this vacuum is not new to her. It has an edge; somewhere in the bottom lid is the distaste. She has seen it lurking in the eyes of all white people. So. The distaste must be for her, her blackness. All things in her are flux and anticipation. But her blackness is static and dread. And it is the blackness that accounts for, that creates, the vacuum edged with distaste in white eyes.

She points her finger at the Mary Janes—a little black shaft of finger, its tip pressed on the display window. The quietly inoffensive assertion of a black child's attempt to communicate with a white adult.

"Them." The word is more sigh than sense.

"What? These? These?" Phlegm and impatience mingle in his voice.

She shakes her head, her fingertip fixed on the spot which, in her view, at any rate, identifies the Mary Janes. He cannot see her view—the angle of his vision, the slant of her finger, makes it incomprehensible to him. His lumpy red hand plops around in the glass casing like the agitated head of a chicken outraged by the loss of its body.

"Christ. Kantcha talk?"

His fingers brush the Mary Janes.

She nods.

"Well, why'nt you say so? One? How many?"

Pecola unfolds her fist, showing the three pennies. He scoots three Mary Janes toward her—three yellow rectangles in each packet. She holds the money toward him. He hesitates, not wanting to touch her hand. She does not know how to move the finger of her right hand from the display counter or how to get the coins out of her left hand. Finally he reaches over and takes the pennies from her hand. His nails graze her damp palm.

Outside, Pecola feels the inexplicable shame ebb.

Dandelions. A dart of affection leaps out from her to them. But they do not look at her and do not send love back. She thinks, "They *are* ugly. They *are* weeds." Preoccupied with that revelation, she trips on the sidewalk crack. Anger stirs and wakes in her; it opens its mouth, and like a hot-mouthed puppy, laps up the dredges of her shame.

Anger is better. There is a sense of being in anger. A reality and presence. An awareness of worth. It is a lovely surging. Her thoughts fall back to Mr. Yacobowski's eyes, his phlegmy voice. The anger will not hold; the puppy is too easily surfeited. Its thirst too quickly quenched, it sleeps. The shame wells up again, its muddy rivulets seeping into her eyes. What to do before the tears come. She remembers the Mary Janes.

Each pale yellow wrapper has a picture on it. A picture of little Mary Jane, for whom the candy is named. Smiling white face. Blond hair in gentle disarray, blue eyes looking at her out of a world of clean comfort. The eyes are petulant, mischievous. To Pecola they are simply pretty. She eats the candy, and its sweetness is good. To eat the candy is somehow to eat the eyes, eat Mary Jane. Love Mary Jane. Be Mary Jane.

Three pennies had bought her nine lovely orgasms with Mary Jane. Lovely Mary Jane, for whom a candy is named.

Three whores lived in the apartment above the Breedloves' storefront. China, Poland, and Miss Marie. Pecola loved them, visited them, and ran their errands. They, in turn, did not despise her.

On an October morning, the morning of the stove-lid triumph, Pecola climbed the stairs to their apartment.

Even before the door was opened to her tapping, she could hear Poland singing—her voice sweet and hard, like new strawberries:

> I got blues in my mealbarrel
> Blues up on the shelf
> I got blues in my mealbarrel
> Blues up on the shelf
> Blues in my bedroom
> 'Cause I'm sleepin' by myself

"Hi, dumplin'. Where your socks?" Marie seldom called Pecola the same thing twice, but invariably her epithets were fond ones chosen from menus and dishes that were forever uppermost in her mind.

"Hello, Miss Marie. Hello, Miss China. Hello, Miss Poland."

"You heard me. Where your socks? You as barelegged as a yard dog."

"I couldn't find any."

"Couldn't find any? Must be somethin' in your house that loves socks."

China chuckled. Whenever something was missing, Marie attributed its disappearance to "something in the house that loved it." "There is somethin' in this house that loves brassieres," she would say with alarm.

Poland and China were getting ready for the evening.

Poland, forever ironing, forever singing. China, sitting on a pale-green kitchen chair, forever and forever curling her hair. Marie never got ready.

The women were friendly, but slow to begin talk. Pecola always took the initiative with Marie, who, once inspired, was difficult to stop.

"How come you got so many boyfriends, Miss Marie?"

"*Boy*friends? *Boy*friends? Chittlin', I ain't seen a *boy* since nineteen and twenty-seven."

"You didn't see none then." China stuck the hot curlers into a tin of Nu Nile hair dressing. The oil hissed at the touch of the hot metal.

"How come, Miss Marie?" Pecola insisted.

"How come what? How come I ain't seen a boy since nineteen and twenty-seven? Because they ain't *been* no boys since then. That's when they stopped. Folks started gettin' born old."

"You mean that's when *you* got old," China said.

"I ain't never got old. Just fat."

"Same thing."

"You think 'cause you skinny, folks think you young? You'd make a haint buy a girdle."

"And you look like the north side of a southbound mule."

"All I know is, them bandy little legs of yours is every bit as old as mine."

"Don't worry 'bout my bandy legs. That's the first thing they push aside."

All three of the women laughed. Marie threw back her head. From deep inside, her laughter came like the sound of many rivers, freely, deeply, muddily, heading for the room of an open sea. China giggled spastically. Each gasp seemed to be yanked out of her by an unseen hand jerking an unseen string. Poland, who seldom spoke unless she was drunk, laughed without sound. When she was sober she hummed mostly or chanted blues songs, of which she knew many.

Pecola fingered the fringe of a scarf that lay on the back of a sofa. "I never seen nobody with as many boyfriends as you got, Miss Marie. How come they all love you?"

Marie opened a bottle of root beer. "What else they gone do? They know I'm rich and good-lookin'. They wants to put their toes in my curly hair, and get at my money."

"You rich, Miss Marie?"

"Puddin', I got money's mammy."

"Where you get it from? You don't do no work."

"Yeah," said China, "where you get it from?"

"Hoover give it me. I did him a favor once, for the F. B. and I."

"What'd you do?"

"I did him a favor. They wanted to catch this crook, you see. Name of Johnny. He was as low-down as they come. . . ."

"We *know* that." China arranged a curl.

". . . the F. B. and I. wanted him bad. He killed more people than TB. And if you *crossed* him? Whoa, Jesus! He'd run you as long as there was ground. Well, I was little and cute then. No more than ninety pounds, soaking wet."

"You ain't never been soaking wet," China said.

"Well, you ain't never been dry. Shut up. Let me tell you, sweetnin'. To tell it true, I was the only one could handle him. He'd go out and rob a bank or kill some people, and I'd say to him, soft-like, 'Johnny, you shouldn't do that.' And he'd say he just had to bring me pretty things. Lacy drawers and all. And every Saturday we'd get a case of beer and fry up some fish. We'd fry it in meal and egg batter, you know, and when it was all brown and crisp—not hard, though—we'd break open that cold beer. . . ." Marie's eyes went soft as the memory of just such a meal sometime, somewhere transfixed her. All her stories were subject to breaking down at descriptions of food. Pecola saw Marie's teeth settling down into the back of crisp sea bass; saw the fat fingers putting back into her mouth tiny flakes of white, hot meat that had escaped from her lips; she heard the "pop" of the beer-bottle cap; smelled the acridness of the first stream of vapor; felt the cold beeriness hit the tongue. She ended the daydream long before Marie.

"But what about the money?" she asked.

China hooted. "She's makin' like she's the Lady in Red that told on Dillinger. Dillinger wouldn't have come near you lessen he was going hunting in Africa and shoot you for a hippo."

"Well, this hippo had a ball back in Chicago. Whoa Jesus, ninety-nine!"

"How come you always say 'Whoa Jesus' and a number?" Pecola had long wanted to know.

"Because my mama taught me never to cuss."

"Did she teach you not to drop your drawers?" China asked.

"Didn't have none," said Marie. "Never saw a pair of drawers till I was fifteen, when I left Jackson and was doing day work in Cincinnati. My white lady gave me some old ones of hers. I thought they was some kind of stocking cap. I put it on my head when I dusted. When she saw me, she liked to fell out."

"You must have been one dumb somebody." China lit a cigarette and cooled her irons.

"How'd I know?" Marie paused. "And what's the use of

putting on something you got to keep taking off all the time? Dewey never let me keep them on long enough to get used to them."

"Dewey who?" This was a somebody new to Pecola.

"Dewey who? Chicken! You never heard me tell of *Dewey?*" Marie was shocked by her negligence.

"No, ma'am."

"Oh, honey, you've missed half your life. Whoa Jesus, one-nine-five. You talkin' 'bout smooth! I met him when I was fourteen. We ran away and lived together like married for three years. You know all those klinker-tops you see runnin' up here? Fifty of 'em in a bowl wouldn't make a Dewey Prince ankle bone. Oh, Lord. How that man loved me!"

China arranged a fingerful of hair into a bang effect. "Then why he left you to sell tail?"

"Girl, when I found out I could sell it—that somebody would pay cold cash for it, you could have knocked me over with a feather."

Poland began to laugh. Soundlessly. "Me too. My auntie whipped me good that first time when I told her I didn't get no money. I said 'Money? For what? He didn't owe me nothin'.' She said, 'The hell he didn't!' "

They all dissolved in laughter.

Three merry gargoyles. Three merry harridans. Amused by a long-ago time of ignorance. They did not belong to those generations of prostitutes created in novels, with great and generous hearts, dedicated, because of the horror of circumstance, to ameliorating the luckless, barren life of men, taking money incidentally and humbly for their "understanding." Nor were they from that sensitive breed of young girl, gone wrong at the hands of fate, forced to culti-

vate an outward brittleness in order to protect her springtime from further shock, but knowing full well she was cut
out for better things, and could make the right man happy.
Neither were they the sloppy, inadequate whores who, unable to make a living at it alone, turn to drug consumption
and traffic or pimps to help complete their scheme of self-
destruction, avoiding suicide only to punish the memory of
some absent father or to sustain the misery of some silent
mother. Except for Marie's fabled love for Dewey Prince,
these women hated men, all men, without shame, apology,
or discrimination. They abused their visitors with a scorn
grown mechanical from use. Black men, white men, Puerto
Ricans, Mexicans, Jews, Poles, whatever—all were inadequate and weak, all came under their jaundiced eyes and
were the recipients of their disinterested wrath. They took
delight in cheating them. On one occasion the town well
knew, they lured a Jew up the stairs, pounced on him, all
three, held him up by the heels, shook everything out of his
pants pockets, and threw him out of the window.

Neither did they have respect for women, who, although
not their colleagues, so to speak, nevertheless deceived their
husbands—regularly or irregularly, it made no difference.
"Sugar-coated whores," they called them, and did not yearn
to be in their shoes. Their only respect was for what they
would have described as "good Christian colored women."
The woman whose reputation was spotless, and who tended
to her family, who didn't drink or smoke or run around.
These women had their undying, if covert, affection. They
would sleep with their husbands, and take their money, but
always with a vengeance.

Nor were they protective and solicitous of youthful innocence. They looked back on their own youth as a period of

ignorance, and regretted that they had not made more of it.
They were not young girls in whores' clothing, or whores
regretting their loss of innocence. They were whores in
whores' clothing, whores who had never been young and
had no word for innocence. With Pecola they were as free
as they were with each other. Marie concocted stories for
her because she was a child, but the stories were breezy and
rough. If Pecola had announced her intention to live the life
they did, they would not have tried to dissuade her or voiced
any alarm.

"You and Dewey Prince have any children, Miss Marie?"

"Yeah. Yeah. We had some." Marie fidgeted. She pulled
a bobby pin from her hair and began to pick her teeth. That
meant she didn't want to talk anymore.

Pecola went to the window and looked down at the empty
street. A tuft of grass had forced its way up through a crack
in the sidewalk, only to meet a raw October wind. She
thought of Dewey Prince and how he loved Miss Marie.
What did love feel like? she wondered. How do grown-ups
act when they love each other? Eat fish together? Into her
eyes came the picture of Cholly and Mrs. Breedlove in bed.
He making sounds as though he were in pain, as though
something had him by the throat and wouldn't let go. Terrible as his noises were, they were not nearly as bad as the
no noise at all from her mother. It was as though she was
not even there. Maybe that was love. Choking sounds and
silence.

Turning her eyes from the window, Pecola looked at the
women.

China had changed her mind about the bangs and was
arranging a small but sturdy pompadour. She was adept in
creating any number of hair styles, but each one left her with

a pinched and harassed look. Then she applied makeup heavily. Now she gave herself surprised eyebrows and a cupid-bow mouth. Later she would make Oriental eyebrows and an evilly slashed mouth.

Poland, in her sweet strawberry voice, began another song:

I know a boy who is sky-soft brown
I know a boy who is sky-soft brown
The dirt leaps for joy when his feet touch the ground.
   His strut is a peacock
   His eye is burning brass
   His smile is sorghum syrup drippin' slow-sweet to
     the last
I know a boy who is sky-soft brown

Marie sat shelling peanuts and popping them into her mouth. Pecola looked and looked at the women. Were they real? Marie belched, softly, purringly, lovingly.

Winter

My daddy's face is a study. Winter moves into it and presides there. His eyes become a cliff of snow threatening to avalanche; his eyebrows bend like black limbs of leafless trees. His skin takes on the pale, cheerless yellow of winter sun; for a jaw he has the edges of a snowbound field dotted with stubble; his high forehead is the frozen sweep of the Erie, hiding currents of gelid thoughts that eddy in darkness. Wolf killer turned hawk fighter, he worked night and day to keep one from the door and the other from under the windowsills. A Vulcan guarding the flames, he gives us instructions about which doors to keep closed or opened for proper distribution of heat, lays kindling by, discusses qualities of coal, and teaches us how to rake, feed, and bank the fire. And he will not unrazor his lips until spring.

Winter tightened our heads with a band of cold and melted our eyes. We put pepper in the feet of our stockings, Vaseline on our faces, and stared through dark icebox mornings at four stewed prunes, slippery lumps of oatmeal, and cocoa with a roof of skin.

But mostly we waited for spring, when there could be gardens.

By the time this winter had stiffened itself into a hateful knot that nothing could loosen, something did loosen it, or rather someone. A someone who splintered the knot into silver threads that tangled us, netted us, made us long for the dull chafe of the previous boredom.

This disrupter of seasons was a new girl in school named Maureen Peal. A high-yellow dream child with long brown hair braided into two lynch ropes that hung down her back. She was rich, at least by our standards, as rich as the richest of the white girls, swaddled in comfort and care. The quality of her clothes threatened to derange Frieda and me. Patent-leather shoes with buckles, a cheaper version of which we got only at Easter and which had disintegrated by the end of May. Fluffy sweaters the color of lemon drops tucked into skirts with pleats so orderly they astounded us. Brightly colored knee socks with white borders, a brown velvet coat trimmed in white rabbit fur, and a matching muff. There was a hint of spring in her sloe green eyes, something summery in her complexion, and a rich autumn ripeness in her walk.

She enchanted the entire school. When teachers called on her, they smiled encouragingly. Black boys didn't trip her in the halls; white boys didn't stone her, white girls didn't suck their teeth when she was assigned to be their work partners; black girls stepped aside when she wanted to use the sink in the girls' toilet, and their eyes genuflected under sliding lids. She never had to search for anybody to eat with in the cafeteria—they flocked to the table of her choice, where she opened fastidious lunches, shaming our jelly-stained bread with egg-salad sandwiches cut into four dainty squares, pink-frosted cupcakes, stocks of celery and carrots, proud, dark apples. She even bought and liked white milk.

Frieda and I were bemused, irritated, and fascinated by her. We looked hard for flaws to restore our equilibrium, but had to be content at first with uglying up her name, changing Maureen Peal to Meringue Pie. Later a minor epiphany was ours when we discovered that she had a dog tooth—a charming one to be sure—but a dog tooth nonetheless. And when we found out that she had been born with six fingers on each hand and that there was a little bump where each extra one had been removed, we smiled. They were small triumphs, but we took what we could get—snickering behind her back and calling her Six-finger-dog-tooth-meringue-pie. But we had to do it alone, for none of the other girls would cooperate with our hostility. They adored her.

When she was assigned a locker next to mine, I could indulge my jealousy four times a day. My sister and I both suspected that we were secretly prepared to be her friend, if she would let us, but I knew it would be a dangerous friendship, for when my eye traced the white border patterns of those Kelly-green knee socks, and felt the pull and slack of my brown stockings, I wanted to kick her. And when I thought of the unearned haughtiness in her eyes, I plotted accidental slammings of locker doors on her hand.

As locker friends, however, we got to know each other a little, and I was even able to hold a sensible conversation with her without visualizing her fall off a cliff, or giggling my way into what I thought was a clever insult.

One day, while I waited at the locker for Frieda, she joined me.

"Hi."

"Hi."

"Waiting for your sister?"

"Uh-huh."

"Which way do you go home?"

"Down Twenty-first Street to Broadway."

"Why don't you go down Twenty-second Street?"

" 'Cause I live on Twenty-first Street."

"Oh. I can walk that way, I guess. Partly, anyway."

"Free country."

Frieda came toward us, her brown stockings straining at the knees because she had tucked the toe under to hide a hole in the foot.

"Maureen's gonna walk part way with us."

Frieda and I exchanged glances, her eyes begging my restraint, mine promising nothing.

It was a false spring day, which, like Maureen, had pierced the shell of a deadening winter. There were puddles, mud, and an inviting warmth that deluded us. The kind of day on which we draped our coats over our heads, left our galoshes in school, and came down with croup the following day. We always responded to the slightest change in weather, the most minute shifts in time of day. Long before seeds were stirring, Frieda and I were scruffing and poking at the earth, swallowing air, drinking rain. . . .

As we emerged from the school with Maureen, we

began to moult immediately. We put our head scarves in our coat pockets, and our coats on our heads. I was wondering how to maneuver Maureen's fur muff into a gutter when a commotion in the playground distracted us. A group of boys was circling and holding at bay a victim, Pecola Breedlove.

Bay Boy, Woodrow Cain, Buddy Wilson, Junie Bug—like a necklace of semiprecious stones they surrounded her. Heady with the smell of their own musk, thrilled by the easy power of a majority, they gaily harassed her.

"Black e mo. Black e mo. Yadaddsleepsnekked. Black e mo black e mo ya dadd sleeps nekked. Black e mo . . ."

They had extemporized a verse made up of two insults about matters over which the victim had no control: the color of her skin and speculations on the sleeping habits of an adult, wildly fitting in its incoherence. That they themselves were black, or that their own father had similarly relaxed habits was irrelevant. It was their contempt for their own blackness that gave the first insult its teeth. They seemed to have taken all of their smoothly cultivated ignorance, their exquisitely learned self-hatred, their elaborately designed hopelessness and sucked it all up into a fiery cone of scorn that had burned for ages in the hollows of their minds—cooled—and spilled over lips of outrage, consuming whatever was in its path. They danced a macabre ballet around the victim, whom, for their own sake, they were prepared to sacrifice to the flaming pit.

Black e mo Black e mo Ya daddy sleeps nekked.
Stch ta ta stch ta ta
stach ta ta ta ta ta

Pecola edged around the circle crying. She had dropped her notebook, and covered her eyes with her hands.

We watched, afraid they might notice us and turn their energies our way. Then Frieda, with set lips and Mama's eyes, snatched her coat from her head and threw it on the ground. She ran toward them and brought her books down on Woodrow Cain's head. The circle broke. Woodrow Cain grabbed his head.

"Hey, girl!"

"You cut that out, you hear?" I had never heard Frieda's voice so loud and clear.

Maybe because Frieda was taller than he was, maybe because he saw her eyes, maybe because he had lost interest in the game, or maybe because he had a crush on Frieda, in any case Woodrow looked frightened just long enough to give her more courage.

"Leave her 'lone, or I'm gone tell everybody what you did!"

Woodrow did not answer; he just walled his eyes.

Bay Boy piped up, "Go on, gal! Ain't nobody bothering you."

"You shut up, Bullet Head." I had found my tongue.

"Who you calling Bullet Head?"

"I'm calling you Bullet Head, Bullet Head."

Frieda took Pecola's hand. "Come on."

"You want a fat lip?" Bay Boy drew back his fist at me.

"Yeah. Gimme one of yours."

"You gone get one."

Maureen appeared at my elbow, and the boys seemed reluctant to continue under her springtime eyes so wide with interest. They buckled in confusion, not willing to beat up three girls under her watchful gaze. So they listened to a budding male instinct that told them to pretend we were unworthy of their attention.

"Come on, man."

"Yeah. Come on. We ain't got time to fool with them."

Grumbling a few disinterested epithets, they moved away.

I picked up Pecola's notebook and Frieda's coat, and the four of us left the playground.

"Old Bullet Head, he's always picking on girls."

Frieda agreed with me. "Miss Forrester said he was incorrigival."

"Really?" I didn't know what that meant, but it had enough of a doom sound in it to be true of Bay Boy.

While Frieda and I clucked on about the near fight, Maureen, suddenly animated, put her velvet-sleeved arm through Pecola's and began to behave as though they were the closest of friends.

"I just moved here. My name is Maureen Peal. What's yours?"

"Pecola."

"Pecola? Wasn't that the name of the girl in *Imitation of Life?*"

"I don't know. What is that?"

"The picture show, you know. Where this mulatto girl hates her mother cause she is black and ugly but then cries at the funeral. It was real sad. Everybody cries in it. Claudette Colbert too."

"Oh." Pecola's voice was no more than a sigh.

"Anyway, her name was Pecola too. She was so pretty. When it comes back, I'm going to see it again. My mother has seen it four times."

Frieda and I walked behind them, surprised at Maureen's friendliness to Pecola, but pleased. Maybe she wasn't so bad, after all. Frieda had put her coat back on her head, and the two of us, so draped, trotted along enjoying the warm breeze and Frieda's heroics.

"You're in my gym class, aren't you?" Maureen asked Pecola.

"Yes."

"Miss Erkmeister's legs sure are bow. I bet she thinks they're cute. How come she gets to wear real shorts, and we have to wear those old bloomers? I want to die every time I put them on."

Pecola smiled but did not look at Maureen.

"Hey." Maureen stopped short. "There's an Isaley's. Want some ice cream? I have money."

She unzipped a hidden pocket in her muff and pulled out a multifolded dollar bill. I forgave her those knee socks.

"My uncle sued Isaley's," Maureen said to the three of us. "He sued the Isaley's in Akron. They said he was disorderly and that that was why they wouldn't serve him, but a friend of his, a policeman, came in and beared the witness, so the suit went through."

"What's a suit?"

"It's when you can beat them up if you want to and won't anybody do nothing. Our family does it all the time. We believe in suits."

At the entrance to Isaley's Maureen turned to Frieda and me, asking, "You all going to buy some ice cream?"

We looked at each other. "No," Frieda said.

Maureen disappeared into the store with Pecola.

Frieda looked placidly down the street; I opened my mouth, but quickly closed it. It was extremely important that the world not know that I fully expected Maureen to buy us some ice cream, that for the past 120 seconds I had been selecting the flavor, that I had begun to like Maureen, and that neither of us had a penny.

We supposed Maureen was being nice to Pecola because of the boys, and were embarrassed to be caught—even by each other—thinking that she would treat us, or that we deserved it as much as Pecola did.

The girls came out. Pecola with two dips of orange-pineapple, Maureen with black raspberry.

"You should have got some," she said. "They had all kinds. Don't eat down to the tip of the cone," she advised Pecola.

"Why?"

"Because there's a fly in there."

"How you know?"

"Oh, not really. A girl told me she found one in the bottom of hers once, and ever since then she throws that part away."

"Oh."

We passed the Dreamland Theater, and Betty Grable smiled down at us.

"Don't you just love her?" Maureen asked.

"Uh-huh," said Pecola.

I differed. "Hedy Lamarr is better."

Maureen agreed. "Ooooo yes. My mother told me that a girl named Audrey, she went to the beauty parlor where we lived before, and asked the lady to fix her hair like Hedy Lamarr's, and the lady said, 'Yeah, when you grow some hair like Hedy Lamarr's.' " She laughed long and sweet.

"Sounds crazy," said Frieda.

"She sure is. Do you know she doesn't even menstrate yet, and she's sixteen. Do you, yet?"

"Yes." Pecola glanced at us.

"So do I." Maureen made no attempt to disguise her pride. "Two months ago I started. My girl friend in Toledo, where we lived before, said when she started she was scared to death. Thought she had killed herself."

"Do you know what it's for?" Pecola asked the question as though hoping to provide the answer herself.

"For babies." Maureen raised two pencil-stroke eyebrows at the obviousness of the question. "Babies need blood when they are inside you, and if you are having a baby, then you don't menstrate. But when you're not having a baby, then you don't have to save the blood, so it comes out."

"How do babies get the blood?" asked Pecola.

"Through the like-line. You know. Where your belly button is. That is where the like-line grows from and pumps the blood to the baby."

"Well, if the belly buttons are to grow like-lines to give the baby blood, and only girls have babies, how come boys have belly buttons?"

Maureen hesitated. "I don't know," she admitted. "But boys have all sorts of things they don't need." Her tinkling laughter was somehow stronger than our nervous ones. She curled her tongue around the edge of the cone, scooping up a dollop of purple that made my eyes water. We were waiting for a stop light to change. Maureen kept scooping the ice cream from around the cone's edge with her tongue; she didn't bite the edge as I would have done. Her tongue circled the cone. Pecola had finished hers; Maureen evidently liked her things to last. While I was thinking about her ice cream, she must have been thinking about her last remark, for she said to Pecola, "Did you ever see a naked man?"

Pecola blinked, then looked away. "No. Where would I see a naked man?"

"I don't know. I just asked."

"I wouldn't even look at him, even if I did see him. That's dirty. Who wants to see a naked man?" Pecola was agitated. "Nobody's father would be naked in front of his own daughter. Not unless he was dirty too."

"I didn't say 'father.' I just said 'a naked man.' "

"Well . . ."

"How come you said 'father'?" Maureen wanted to know.

"Who else would she see, dog tooth?" I was glad to have a chance to show anger. Not only because of the ice cream, but because we had seen our own father naked and didn't care to be reminded of it and feel the shame brought on by the absence of shame. He had been walking down the hall from the bathroom into his bedroom and passed the open door of our room. We had lain there wide-eyed. He stopped and looked in, trying to see in the dark room whether we were really asleep—or was it his imagination that opened eyes were looking at him? Apparently he convinced himself that we were sleeping. He moved away, confident that his little girls would not lie open-eyed like that, staring, staring. When he had moved on, the dark took only him away, not his nakedness. That stayed in the room with us. Friendly-like.

"I'm not talking to you," said Maureen. "Besides, I don't care if she sees her father naked. She can look at him all day if she wants to. Who cares?"

"You do," said Frieda. "That's all you talk about."

"It is not."

"It is so. Boys, babies, and somebody's naked daddy. You must be boy-crazy."

"You better be quiet."

"Who's gonna make me?" Frieda put her hand on her hip and jutted her face toward Maureen.

"You all ready made. Mammy made."

"You stop talking about my mama."

"Well, you stop talking about my daddy."

"Who said anything about your old daddy?"

"You did."

"Well, you started it."

"I wasn't even talking to you. I was talking to Pecola."

"Yeah. About seeing her naked daddy."

"So what if she did see him?"

Pecola shouted, "I never saw my daddy naked. Never."

"You did too," Maureen snapped. "Bay Boy said so."

"I did not."

"You did."

"I did not."

"Did. Your own daddy, too!"

Pecola tucked her head in—a funny, sad, helpless movement. A kind of hunching of the shoulders, pulling in of the neck, as though she wanted to cover her ears.

"You stop talking about her daddy," I said.

"What do I care about her old black daddy?" asked Maureen.

"Black? Who you calling black?"

"You!"

"You think you so cute!" I swung at her and missed, hitting Pecola in the face. Furious at my clumsiness, I threw my notebook at her, but it caught her in the small of her velvet back, for she had turned and was flying across the street against traffic.

Safe on the other side, she screamed at us, "I *am* cute! And you ugly! Black and ugly black e mos. I *am* cute!"

She ran down the street, the green knee socks making her legs look like wild dandelion stems that had somehow lost their heads. The weight of her remark stunned us, and it was a second or two before Frieda and I collected ourselves enough to shout, "Six-finger-dog-tooth-meringue-pie!" We chanted this most powerful of our arsenal of insults as long as we could see the green stems and rabbit fur.

Grown people frowned at the three girls on the curbside, two with their coats draped over their heads, the collars framing the eyebrows like nuns' habits, black garters showing where they bit the tops of brown stockings that barely covered the knees, angry faces knotted like dark cauliflowers.

Pecola stood a little apart from us, her eyes hinged in the direction in which Maureen had fled. She seemed to fold into herself, like a pleated wing. Her pain antagonized me. I wanted to open her up, crisp her edges, ram a stick down that hunched and curving spine, force her to stand erect and spit the misery out on the streets. But she held it in where it could lap up into her eyes.

Frieda snatched her coat from her head. "Come on, Claudia. 'Bye, Pecola."

We walked quickly at first, and then slower, pausing every now and then to fasten garters, tie shoelaces, scratch, or examine old scars. We were sinking under the wisdom, accuracy, and relevance of Maureen's last words. If she was cute—and if anything could be believed, she *was*—then we were not. And what did that mean? We were lesser. Nicer, brighter, but still lesser. Dolls we could destroy, but we could not destroy the honey voices of parents and aunts, the obedience in the eyes of our peers, the slippery light in the eyes of our teachers when they encountered the Maureen Peals of the world. What was the secret? What did we lack? Why was it important? And so what? Guileless and without vanity, we were still in love with ourselves then. We felt comfortable in our skins, enjoyed the news that our senses released to us, admired our dirt, cultivated our scars, and could not comprehend this unworthiness. Jealousy we understood and thought natural—a desire to have what somebody else had; but envy was a strange, new feeling for us. And all the time we knew that Maureen Peal was not the Enemy and not worthy of such intense hatred. The *Thing* to fear was the *Thing* that made *her* beautiful, and not us.

The house was quiet when we opened the door. The acrid smell of simmering turnips filled our cheeks with sour saliva.

"Mama!"

There was no answer, but a sound of feet. Mr. Henry shuffled part of the way down the stairs. One thick, hairless leg leaned out of his bathrobe.

"Hello there, Greta Garbo; hello, Ginger Rogers."

We gave him the giggle he was accustomed to. "Hello, Mr. Henry. Where's Mama?"

"She went to your grandmaw's. Left word for you to cut off the turnips and eat some graham crackers till she got back. They in the kitchen."

We sat in silence at the kitchen table, crumbling the crackers into anthills. In a little while Mr. Henry came back down the stairs. Now he had his trousers on under his robe.

"Say. Wouldn't you all like some cream?"

"Oh, yes, sir."

"Here. Here's a quarter. Gone over to Isaley's and get yourself some cream. You been good girls, ain't you?"

His light-green words restored color to the day. "Yes, sir. Thank you, Mr. Henry. Will you tell Mama for us if she comes?"

"Sure. But she ain't due back for a spell."

Coatless, we left the house and had gotten all the way to the corner when Frieda said, "I don't want to go to Isaley's."

"What?"

"I don't want ice cream. I want potato chips."

"They got potato chips at Isaley's."

"I know, but why go all that long way? Miss Bertha got potato chips."

"But I want ice cream."

"No you don't, Claudia."

"I do too."

"Well, you go on to Isaley's. I'm going to Miss Bertha's."

"But you got the quarter, and I don't want to go all the way up there by myself."

"Then let's go to Miss Bertha's. You like her candy, don't you?"

"It's always stale, and she always runs out of stuff."

"Today is Friday. She orders fresh on Friday."

"And then that crazy old Soaphead Church lives there."

"So what? We're together. We'll run if he does anything at us."

"He scares me."

"Well, I don't want to go up by Isaley's. Suppose Meringue Pie is hanging around. You want to run into her, Claudia?"

"Come on, Frieda. I'll get candy."

Miss Bertha had a small candy, snuff, and tobacco store. One brick room sitting in her front yard. You had to peep in the door, and if she wasn't there, you knocked on the door of her house in back. This day she was sitting behind the counter reading a Bible in a tube of sunlight.

Frieda bought potato chips, and we got three Powerhouse bars for ten cents, and had a dime left. We hurried back home to sit under the lilac bushes on the side of the house. We always did our Candy Dance there so Rosemary could see us and get jealous. The Candy Dance was a humming, skipping, foot-tapping, eating, smacking combination that overtook us when we had sweets. Creeping between the bushes and the side of the house, we heard voices and laughter. We looked into the living-room window, expecting to see Mama. Instead we saw Mr. Henry and two women. In a playful manner, the way grandmothers do with babies, he was sucking the fingers of one of the women, whose laughter filled a tiny place over his head. The other woman was buttoning her coat. We knew immediately who they were, and our flesh crawled. One was China, and the other was called the Maginot Line. The back of my neck itched. These were the fancy women of the maroon nail polish that Mama and Big Mama hated. And in our house.

China was not too terrible, at least not in our imaginations. She was thin, aging, absentminded, and unaggressive. But the Maginot Line. That was the one my mother said she "wouldn't let eat out of one of her plates." That was the one church women never allowed their eyes to rest on. That was the one who had killed people, set them on fire, poisoned them, cooked them in lye. Although I thought the Maginot Line's face, hidden under all that fat, was really sweet, I had heard too many black and red words about her, seen too many mouths go triangle at the mention of her name, to dwell on any redeeming features she might have.

Showing brown teeth, China seemed to be genuinely enjoying Mr. Henry. The sight of him licking her fingers brought to mind the girlie magazines in his room. A cold wind blew somewhere in me, lifting little leaves of terror and obscure longing. I thought I saw a mild lonesomeness cross the face of the Maginot Line. But it may have been my own image that I saw in the slow flaring of her nostrils, in her eyes that reminded me of waterfalls in movies about Hawaii.

The Maginot Line yawned and said, "Come on, China. We can't hang in here all day. Them people be home soon." She moved toward the door.

Frieda and I dropped down to the ground, looking wildly into each other's eyes. When the women were some distance away, we went inside. Mr. Henry was in the kitchen opening a bottle of pop.

"Back already?"

"Yes, sir."

"Cream all gone?" His little teeth looked so kindly and helpless. Was that really our Mr. Henry with China's fingers?

"We got candy instead."

"You did huh? Ole sugar-tooth Greta Garbo."

He wiped the bottle sweat and turned it up to his lips—a gesture that made me uncomfortable.

"Who were those women, Mr. Henry?"

He choked on the pop and looked at Frieda. "What you say?"

"Those women," she repeated, "who just left. Who were they?"

"Oh." He laughed the grown-up getting-ready-to-lie laugh. A heh-heh we knew well.

"Those were some members of my Bible class. We read the scriptures together, and so they came today to read with me."

"Oh," said Frieda. I was looking at his house slippers to keep from seeing those kindly teeth frame a lie. He walked toward the stairs and then turned back to us.

"Bed' not mention it to your mother. She don't take to

so much Bible study and don't like me having visitors, even if they good Christians."

"No, sir, Mr. Henry. We won't."

He rapidly mounted the stairs.

"Should we?" I asked. "Tell Mama?"

Frieda sighed. She had not even opened her Powerhouse bar or her potato chips, and now she traced the letters on the candy wrappers with her fingers. Suddenly she lifted her head and began to look all around the kitchen.

"No. I guess not. No plates are out."

"Plates? What you talking about now?"

"No plates are out. The Maginot Line didn't eat out of one of Mama's plates. Besides, Mama would just fuss all day if we told her."

We sat down and looked at the graham-cracker anthills we had made.

"We better cut off the turnips. They'll burn, and Mama will whip us," she said.

"I know."

"But if we let them burn, we won't have to eat them."

"Heyyy, what a lovely idea," I thought.

"Which you want? A whipping and no turnips, or turnips and no whippings?"

"I don't know. Maybe we could burn them just a little so Mama and Daddy can eat them, but we can say we can't."

"O.K."

I made a volcano out of my anthill.

"Frieda?"

"What?"

"What did Woodrow do that you was gonna tell?"

"Wet the bed. Mrs. Cain told Mama he won't quit."

"Old nasty."

The sky was getting dark; I looked out of the window and saw snow falling. I poked my finger down into the mouth of my volcano, and it toppled, dispersing the golden grains into little swirls. The turnip pot crackled.

*SEETHECATITGOESMEOWMEOWCOM
EANDPLAYCOMEPLAYWITHJANETHE
KITTENWILLNOTPLAYPLAYPLAYPLA*

They come from Mobile. Aiken. From Newport News. From Marietta. From Meridian. And the sound of these places in their mouths make you think of love. When you ask them where they are from, they tilt their heads and say "Mobile" and you think you've been kissed. They say "Aiken" and you see a white butterfly glance off a fence with a torn wing. They say "Nagadoches" and you want to say "Yes, I will." You don't know what these towns are like, but you love what happens to the air when they open their lips and let the names ease out.

Meridian. The sound of it opens the windows of a room like the first four notes of a hymn. Few people can say the names of their home towns with such sly affection. Perhaps because they don't have home towns, just places where they were born. But these girls soak up the juice of their home towns, and it never leaves them. They are thin brown girls who have looked long at hollyhocks in the backyards of Meridian, Mobile, Aiken, and Baton Rouge. And like hollyhocks they are narrow, tall, and still. Their roots are deep, their stalks are firm, and only the top blossom nods in the wind. They have the eyes of people who can tell what time it is by the color of the sky. Such girls live in quiet black neighborhoods where everybody is gainfully employed. Where there are porch swings hanging from chains. Where the grass is cut with a scythe, where rooster combs and sunflowers grow in the yards, and pots of bleeding heart, ivy, and mother-in-law tongue line the steps and window-sills. Such girls have bought watermelon and snapbeans from the fruit man's wagon. They have put in the window the cardboard sign that has a pound measure printed on each of three edges—10 lbs., 25 lbs., 50 lbs.—and NO ICE on the fourth. These particular brown girls from Mobile and Aiken are not like some of their sisters. They are not fretful, nervous, or shrill; they do not have lovely black necks that stretch as though against an invisible collar; their eyes do not bite. These sugar-brown Mobile girls move through the streets without a stir. They are as sweet and plain as butter-cake. Slim ankles; long, narrow feet. They wash themselves with orange-colored Lifebuoy soap, dust themselves with Cashmere Bouquet talc, clean their teeth with salt on a piece of rag, soften their skin with Jergens Lotion. They smell like wood, newspapers, and vanilla. They straighten their hair with Dixie Peach, and part it on the side. At night they curl it in paper from brown bags, tie a print scarf around their heads, and sleep with hands folded across their stomachs. They do not drink, smoke, or swear, and they still call sex "nookey." They sing second soprano in the choir, and al-though their voices are clear and steady, they are never picked to solo. They are in the second row, white blouses starched, blue skirts almost purple from ironing.

They go to land-grant colleges, normal schools, and learn how to do the white man's work with refinement: home economics to prepare his food; teacher education to instruct black children in obedience; music to soothe the weary master and entertain his blunted soul. Here they learn the rest of the lesson begun in those soft houses with porch swings and pots of bleeding heart: how to behave. The careful development of thrift, patience, high morals, and good manners. In short, how to get rid of the funkiness. The dreadful funkiness of passion, the funkiness of nature, the funkiness of the wide range of human emotions.

Wherever it erupts, this Funk, they wipe it away; where it crusts, they dissolve it; wherever it drips, flowers, or clings, they find it and fight it until it dies. They fight this battle all the way to the grave. The laugh that is a little too loud; the enunciation a little too round; the gesture a little too generous. They hold their behind in for fear of a sway too free; when they wear lipstick, they never cover the entire mouth for fear of lips too thick, and they worry, worry, worry about the edges of their hair.

They never seem to have boyfriends, but they always marry. Certain men watch them, without seeming to, and know that if such a girl is in his house, he will sleep on sheets boiled white, hung out to dry on juniper bushes, and pressed flat with a heavy iron. There will be pretty paper flowers decorating the picture of his mother, a large Bible in the front room. They feel secure. They know their work clothes will be mended, washed, and ironed on Monday, that their Sunday shirts will billow on hangers from the door jamb, stiffly starched and white. They look at her hands and know what she will do with biscuit dough; they smell the coffee and the fried ham; see the white, smoky grits with a dollop of butter on top. Her hips assure them that she will bear children easily and painlessly. And they are right.

What they do not know is that this plain brown girl will build her nest stick by stick, make it her own inviolable world, and stand guard over its every plant, weed, and doily, even against him. In silence will she return the lamp to where she put it in the first place; remove the dishes from the table as soon as the last bite is taken; wipe the doorknob after a greasy hand has touched it. A sidelong look will be enough to tell him to smoke on the back porch. Children will sense instantly that they cannot come into her yard to retrieve a ball. But the men do not know these things. Nor do they know that she will give him her body sparingly and partially. He must enter her surreptitiously, lifting the hem of her nightgown only to her navel. He must rest his weight on his elbows when they make love, ostensibly to avoid hurting her breasts but actually to keep her from having to touch or feel too much of him.

While he moves inside her, she will wonder why they didn't put the necessary but private parts of the body in some more convenient place—like the armpit, for example, or the palm of the hand. Someplace one could get to easily, and quickly, without undressing. She stiffens when she feels one of her paper curlers coming undone from the activity of love; imprints in her mind which one it is that is coming loose so she can quickly secure it once he is through. She hopes he will not sweat—the damp may get into her hair; and that she will remain dry between her legs—she hates the glucking sound they make when she is moist. When she senses some spasm about to grip him, she will make rapid movements with her hips, press her fingernails into his back, suck in her breath, and pretend she is having an orgasm. She might wonder again, for the six hundredth time, what it would be like to have *that* feeling while her husband's penis is inside her. The closest thing to it was the time she was walking down the street and her napkin slipped free of her sanitary belt. It moved gently between her legs as she walked. Gently, ever so gently. And then a slight and distinctly delicious sensation collected in her crotch. As the delight grew, she had to stop in the street, hold her thighs together to contain it. That must be what it is like, she thinks, but it never happens while he is inside her. When he withdraws, she pulls her nightgown down, slips out of the bed and into the bathroom with relief.

Occasionally some living thing will engage her affections. A cat, perhaps, who will love her order, precision, and constancy; who will be as clean and quiet as she is. The cat will settle quietly on the windowsill and caress her with his eyes. She can hold him in her arms, letting his back paws struggle for footing on her breast and his forepaws cling to her shoulder. She can rub the smooth fur and feel the unresisting flesh underneath. At her gentlest touch he will preen, stretch, and open his mouth. And she will accept the strangely pleasant sensation that comes when he writhes beneath her hand and flattens his eyes with a surfeit of sensual delight. When she stands cooking at the table, he will circle about her shanks, and the trill of his fur spirals up her legs to her thighs, to make her fingers tremble a little in the pie dough.

Or, as she sits reading the "Uplifting Thoughts" in *The Liberty Magazine*, the cat will jump into her lap. She will fondle that soft hill of hair and let the warmth of the animal's body seep over and into the deeply private areas of her lap. Sometimes the magazine drops, and she opens her legs just a little, and the two of them will be still together, perhaps shifting a little together, sleeping a little together, until four o'clock, when the intruder comes home from work vaguely anxious about what's for dinner.

The cat will always know that he is first in her affections. Even after she bears a child. For she does bear a child— easily, and painlessly. But only one. A son. Named Junior.

One such girl from Mobile, or Meridian, or Aiken who did not sweat in her armpits nor between her thighs, who smelled of wood and vanilla, who had made soufflés in the Home Economics Department, moved with her husband, Louis, to Lorain, Ohio. Her name was Geraldine. There she built her nest, ironed shirts, potted bleeding hearts, played with her cat, and birthed Louis Junior.

Geraldine did not allow her baby, Junior, to cry. As long as his needs were physical, she could meet them—comfort and satiety. He was always brushed, bathed, oiled, and shod. Geraldine did not talk to him, coo to him, or indulge him in kissing bouts, but she saw that every other desire was fulfilled. It was not long before the child discovered the difference in his mother's behavior to himself and the cat. As he grew older, he learned how to direct his hatred of his mother to the cat, and spent some happy moments watching it suffer. The cat survived, because Geraldine was seldom away from home, and could effectively soothe the animal when Junior abused him.

Geraldine, Louis, Junior, and the cat lived next to the playground of Washington Irving School. Junior considered the playground his own, and the schoolchildren coveted his freedom to sleep late, go home for lunch, and dominate the playground after school. He hated to see the swings, slides, monkey bars, and seesaws empty and tried to get kids to stick around as long as possible. White kids; his mother did not like him to play with niggers. She had explained to him the difference between colored people and niggers. They were easily identifiable. Colored people were neat and quiet; niggers were dirty and loud. He belonged to the former group: he wore white shirts and blue trousers; his hair was cut as close to his scalp as possible to avoid any suggestion of wool, the part was etched into his hair by the barber. In winter his mother put Jergens Lotion on his face to keep the skin from becoming ashen. Even though he was light-skinned, it was possible to ash. The line between colored and nigger was not always clear; subtle and telltale signs threatened to erode it, and the watch had to be constant.

Junior used to long to play with the black boys. More than anything in the world he wanted to play King of the Mountain and have them push him down the mound of dirt and roll over him. He wanted to feel their hardness pressing on him, smell their wild blackness, and say "Fuck you" with that lovely casualness. He wanted to sit with them on curb-stones and compare the sharpness of jackknives, the distance and arcs of spitting. In the toilet he wanted to share with them the laurels of being able to pee far and long. Bay Boy and P. L. had at one time been his idols. Gradually he came to agree with his mother that neither Bay Boy nor P. L. was good enough for him. He played only with Ralph Nisensky, who was two years younger, wore glasses, and didn't want to *do* anything. More and more Junior enjoyed bullying girls. It was easy making them scream and run. How he laughed when they fell down and their bloomers showed. When they got up, their faces red and crinkled, it made him feel good. The nigger girls he did not pick on very much. They usually traveled in packs, and once when he threw a stone at some of them, they chased, caught, and beat him witless. He lied to his mother, saying Bay Boy did it. His mother was very upset. His father just kept on reading the Lorain *Journal*.

When the mood struck him, he would call a child passing by to come play on the swings or the seesaw. If the child wouldn't, or did and left too soon, Junior threw gravel at him. He became a very good shot.

Alternately bored and frightened at home, the playground was his joy. On a day when he had been especially idle, he saw a very black girl taking a shortcut through the playground. She kept her head down as she walked. He had seen her many times before, standing alone, always alone, at recess. Nobody ever played with her. Probably, he thought, because she was ugly.

Now Junior called to her. "Hey! What are you doing walking through my yard?"

The girl stopped.

"Nobody can come through this yard 'less I say so."

"This ain't your yard. It's the school's."

"But I'm in charge of it."

The girl started to walk away.

"Wait." Junior walked toward her. "You can play in it if you want to. What's your name?"

"Pecola. I don't want to play."

"Come on. I'm not going to bother you."

"I got to go home."

"Say, you want to see something? I got something to show you."

"No. What is it?"

"Come on in my house. See, I live right there. Come on. I'll show you."

"Show me what?"

"Some kittens. We got some kittens. You can have one if you want."

"Real kittens?"

"Yeah. Come on."

He pulled gently at her dress. Pecola began to move toward his house. When he knew she had agreed, Junior ran ahead excitedly, stopping only to yell back at her to come on. He held the door open for her, smiling his encouragement. Pecola climbed the porch stairs and hesitated there, afraid to follow him. The house looked dark. Junior said, "There's nobody here. My ma's gone out, and my father's at work. Don't you want to see the kittens?"

Junior turned on the lights. Pecola stepped inside the door.

How beautiful, she thought. What a beautiful house. There was a big red-and-gold Bible on the dining-room table. Little lace doilies were everywhere—on arms and backs of chairs, in the center of a large dining table, on little tables. Potted plants were on all the windowsills. A color picture of Jesus Christ hung on a wall with the prettiest paper flowers fastened on the frame. She wanted to see everything slowly, slowly. But Junior kept saying, "Hey, you. Come on. Come on." He pulled her into another room, even more beautiful than the first. More doilies, a big lamp with green-and-gold base and white shade. There was even a rug on the floor, with enormous dark-red flowers. She was deep in admiration of the flowers when Junior said, "Here!" Pecola turned. "Here is your kitten!" he screeched. And he threw a big black cat right in her face. She sucked in her breath in fear and surprise and felt fur in her mouth. The cat clawed her face and chest in an effort to right itself, then leaped nimbly to the floor.

Junior was laughing and running around the room clutching his stomach delightedly. Pecola touched the scratched place on her face and felt tears coming. When she started toward the doorway, Junior leaped in front of her.

"You can't get out. You're my prisoner," he said. His eyes were merry but hard.

"You let me go."

"No!" He pushed her down, ran out the door that separated the rooms, and held it shut with his hands. Pecola's banging on the door increased his gasping, high-pitched laughter.

The tears came fast, and she held her face in her hands. When something soft and furry moved around her ankles, she jumped, and saw it was the cat. He wound himself in and about her legs. Momentarily distracted from her fear, she squatted down to touch him, her hands wet from the tears. The cat rubbed up against her knee. He was black all over, deep silky black, and his eyes, pointing down toward his nose, were bluish green. The light made them shine like blue ice. Pecola rubbed the cat's head; he whined, his tongue flicking with pleasure. The blue eyes in the black face held her.

Junior, curious at not hearing her sobs, opened the door, and saw her squatting down rubbing the cat's back. He saw the cat stretching its head and flattening its eyes. He had seen that expression many times as the animal responded to his mother's touch.

"Gimme my cat!" His voice broke. With a movement both awkward and sure he snatched the cat by one of its hind legs and began to swing it around his head in a circle.

"Stop that!" Pecola was screaming. The cat's free paws were stiffened, ready to grab anything to restore balance, its mouth wide, its eyes blue streaks of horror.

Still screaming, Pecola reached for Junior's hand. She heard her dress rip under her arm. Junior tried to push her away, but she grabbed the arm which was swinging the cat. They both fell, and in falling, Junior let go the cat, which, having been released in mid-motion, was thrown full force against the window. It slithered down and fell on the radiator behind the sofa. Except for a few shudders, it was still. There was only the slightest smell of singed fur.

Geraldine opened the door.

"What is this?" Her voice was mild, as though asking a perfectly reasonable question. "Who is this girl?"

"She killed our cat," said Junior. "Look." He pointed to the radiator, where the cat lay, its blue eyes closed, leaving only an empty, black, and helpless face.

Geraldine went to the radiator and picked up the cat. He was limp in her arms, but she rubbed her face in his fur. She looked at Pecola. Saw the dirty torn dress, the plaits sticking out on her head, hair matted where the plaits had come undone, the muddy shoes with the wad of gum peeping out from between the cheap soles, the soiled socks, one of which had been walked down into the heel of the shoe. She saw the safety pin holding the hem of the dress up. Up over the hump of the cat's back she looked at her. She had seen this little girl all of her life. Hanging out of windows over saloons in Mobile, crawling over the porches of shotgun houses on the edge of town, sitting in bus stations holding paper bags and crying to mothers who kept saying "Shet up!" Hair uncombed, dresses falling apart, shoes untied and caked with dirt. They had stared at her with great uncomprehending eyes. Eyes that questioned nothing and asked everything. Unblinking and unabashed, they stared up at her. The end of the world lay in their eyes, and the beginning, and all the waste in between.

They were everywhere. They slept six in a bed, all their pee mixing together in the night as they wet their beds each in his own candy-and-potato-chip dream. In the long, hot days, they idled away, picking plaster from the walls and digging into the earth with sticks. They sat in little rows on street curbs, crowded into pews at church, taking space from the nice, neat, colored children; they clowned on the playgrounds, broke things in dime stores, ran in front of you on the street, made ice slides on the sloped sidewalks in winter. The girls grew up knowing nothing of girdles, and the boys announced their manhood by turning the bills of their caps backward. Grass wouldn't grow where they lived. Flowers died. Shades fell down. Tin cans and tires blossomed where they lived. They lived on cold black-eyed peas and orange pop. Like flies they hovered; like flies they settled. And this one had settled in her house. Up over the hump of the cat's back she looked.

"Get out," she said, her voice quiet. "You nasty little black bitch. Get out of my house."

The cat shuddered and flicked his tail.

Pecola backed out of the room, staring at the pretty milk-brown lady in the pretty gold-and-green house who was talking to her through the cat's fur. The pretty lady's words made the cat fur move; the breath of each word parted the fur. Pecola turned to find the front door and saw Jesus looking down at her with sad and unsurprised eyes, his long brown hair parted in the middle, the gay paper flowers twisted around his face.

Outside, the March wind blew into the rip in her dress. She held her head down against the cold. But she could not hold it low enough to avoid seeing the snowflakes falling and dying on the pavement.

Spring

The first twigs are thin, green, and supple. They bend into a complete circle, but will not break. Their delicate, showy hopefulness shooting from forsythia and lilac bushes meant only a change in whipping style. They beat us differently in the spring. Instead of the dull pain of a winter strap, there were these new green switches that lost their sting long after the whipping was over. There was a nervous meanness in these long twigs that made us long for the steady stroke of a strap or the firm but honest slap of a hairbrush. Even now spring for me is shot through with the remembered ache of switchings, and forsythia holds no cheer.

Sunk in the grass of an empty lot on a spring Saturday, I split the stems of milkweed and thought about ants and peach pits and death and where the world went when I closed my eyes. I must have lain long in the grass, for the shadow that was in front of me when I left the house had disappeared when I went back. I entered the house, as the house was bursting with an uneasy quiet. Then I heard my mother singing something about trains and Arkansas. She came in the back door with some folded yellow curtains which she piled on the kitchen table. I sat down on the floor to listen to the song's story, and noticed how strangely she was behaving. She still had her hat on, and her shoes were dusty, as though she had been walking in deep dirt. She put on some water to boil and then swept the porch; then she hauled out the curtain stretcher, but instead of putting the damp curtains on it, she swept the porch again. All the time singing about trains and Arkansas.

When she finished, I went to look for Frieda. I found her upstairs lying on our bed, crying the tired, whimpering cry that follows the first wailings—mostly gasps and shudderings. I lay on the bed and looked at the tiny bunches of wild roses sprinkled over her dress. Many washings had faded their color and dimmed their outlines.

"What happened, Frieda?"

She lifted a swollen face from the crook of her arm. Shuddering still, she sat up, letting her thin legs dangle over the bedside. I knelt on the bed and picked up the hem of my dress to wipe her running nose. She never liked wiping noses on clothes, but this time she let me. It was the way Mama did with her apron.

"Did you get a whipping?"

She shook her head no.

"Then why you crying?"

"Because."

"Because what?"

"Mr. Henry."

"What'd he do?"

"Daddy beat him up."

"What for? The Maginot Line? Did he find out about the Maginot Line?"

"No."

"Well, what, then? Come on, Frieda. How come I can't know?"

"He . . . *picked* at me."

"Picked at you? You mean like Soaphead Church?"

"Sort of."

"He showed his privates at you?"

"Noooo. He touched me."

"Where?"

"Here and here." She pointed to the tiny breasts that, like two fallen acorns, scattered a few faded rose leaves on her dress.

"Really? How did it feel?"

"Oh, Claudia." She sounded put-out. I wasn't asking the right questions.

"It didn't feel like anything."

"But wasn't it supposed to? Feel good, I mean?" Frieda sucked her teeth. "What'd he do? Just walk up and pinch them?"

She sighed. "First he said how pretty I was. Then he grabbed my arm and touched me."

"Where was Mama and Daddy?"

"Over at the garden weeding."

"What'd you say when he did it?"

"Nothing. I just ran out the kitchen and went to the garden."

"Mama said we was never to cross the tracks by ourselves."

"Well, what would you do? Set there and let him pinch you?"

I looked at my chest. "I don't have nothing to pinch. I'm never going to have nothing."

"Oh, Claudia, you're jealous of everything. You *want* him to?"

"No, I just get tired of having everything last."

"You do not. What about scarlet fever? You had that first."

"Yes, but it didn't last. Anyway, what happened at the garden?"

"I told Mama, and she told Daddy, and we all come home, and he was gone, so we waited for him, and when Daddy saw him come up on the porch, he threw our old tricycle at his head and knocked him off the porch."

"Did he die?"

"Naw. He got up and started singing 'Nearer My God to Thee.' Then Mama hit him with a broom and told him to keep the Lord's name out of his mouth, but he wouldn't stop, and Daddy was cussing, and everybody was screaming."

"Oh, shoot, I always miss stuff."

"And Mr. Buford came running out with his gun, and Mama told him to go somewhere and sit down, and Daddy said no, give him the gun, and Mr. Buford did, and Mama screamed, and Mr. Henry shut up and started running, and Daddy shot at him and Mr. Henry jumped out of his shoes and kept on running in his socks. Then Rosemary came out and said that Daddy was going to jail, and I hit her."

"Real hard?"

"Real hard."

"Is that when Mama whipped you?"

"She didn't whip me, I told you."

"Then why you crying?"

"Miss Dunion came in after everybody was quiet, and Mama and Daddy was fussing about who let Mr. Henry in anyway, and she said that Mama should take me to the doctor, because I might be ruined, and Mama started screaming all over again."

"At you?"

"No. At Miss Dunion."

"But why were you crying?"

"I don't want to be *ruined!*"

"What's ruined?"

"You know. Like the Maginot Line. She's ruined. Mama said so." The tears came back.

An image of Frieda, big and fat, came to mind. Her thin legs swollen, her face surrounded by layers of rouged skin. I too begin to feel tears.

"But, Frieda, you could exercise and not eat."

She shrugged.

"Besides, what about China and Poland? They're ruined too, aren't they? And they ain't fat."

"That's because they drink whiskey. Mama says whiskey ate them up."

"You could drink whiskey."

"Where would I get whiskey?"

We thought about this. Nobody would sell it to us; we had no money, anyway. There was never any in our house. Who would have some?

"Pecola," I said. "Her father's always drunk. She can get us some."

"You think so?"

"Sure. Cholly's always drunk. Let's go ask her. We don't have to tell her what for."

"Now?"

"Sure, now."

"What'll we tell Mama?"

"Nothing. Let's just go out the back. One at a time. So she won't notice."

"O.K. You go first, Claudia."

We opened the fence gate at the bottom of the backyard and ran down the alley.

Pecola lived on the other side of Broadway. We had never been in her house, but we knew where it was. A two-story gray building that had been a store downstairs and had an apartment upstairs.

Nobody answered our knock on the front door, so we walked around to the side door. As we approached, we heard radio music and looked to see where it came from. Above us was the second-story porch, lined with slanting, rotting rails, and sitting on the porch was the Maginot Line herself. We stared up and automatically reached for the other's hand. A mountain of flesh, she lay rather than sat in a rocking chair. She had no shoes on, and each foot was poked between a railing: tiny baby toes at the tip of puffy feet; swollen ankles smoothed and tightened the skin; massive legs like tree stumps parted wide at the knees, over which spread two roads of soft flabby inner thigh that kissed each other deep in the shade of her dress and closed. A dark-brown root-beer bottle, like a burned limb, grew out of her dimpled hand. She looked at us down through the porch railings and emitted a low, long belch. Her eyes were as clean as rain, and again I remembered the waterfall.

Neither of us could speak. Both of us imagined we were seeing what was to become of Frieda. The Maginot Line smiled at us.

"You all looking for somebody?"

I had to pull my tongue from the roof of my mouth to say, "Pecola—she live here?"

"Uh-huh, but she ain't here now. She gone to her mama's work place to git the wash."

"Yes, ma'am. She coming back?"

"Uh-huh. She got to hang up the clothes before the sun goes down."

"Oh."

"You can wait for her. Wanna come up here and wait?"

We exchanged glances. I looked back up at the broad cinnamon roads that met in the shadow of her dress.

Frieda said, "No, ma'am."

"Well," the Maginot Line seemed interested in our problem. "You can go to her mama's work place, but it's way over by the lake."

"Where by the lake?"

"That big white house with the wheelbarrow full of flowers."

It was a house that we knew, having admired the large white wheelbarrow tilted down on spoked wheels and planted with seasonal flowers.

"Ain't that too far for you all to go walking?"

Frieda scratched her knee.

"Why don't you wait for her? You can come up here. Want some pop?" Those rain-soaked eyes lit up, and her smile was full, not like the pinched and holding-back smile of other grown-ups.

I moved to go up the stairs, but Frieda said, "No, ma'am, we ain't allowed."

I was amazed at her courage, and frightened of her sassiness. The smile of the Maginot Line slipped. "Ain't 'llowed?"

"No'm."

"Ain't 'llowed to what?"

"Go in your house."

"Is that right?" The waterfalls were still. "How come?"

"My mama said so. My mama said you ruined."

The waterfalls began to run again. She put the root-beer bottle to her lips and drank it empty. With a graceful movement of the wrist, a gesture so quick and small we never really saw it, only remembered it afterward, she tossed the bottle over the rail at us. It split at our feet, and shards of brown glass dappled our legs before we could jump back. The Maginot Line put a fat hand on one of the folds of her stomach and laughed. At first just a deep humming with her mouth closed, then a larger, warmer sound. Laughter at once beautiful and frightening. She let her head tilt sideways, closed her eyes, and shook her massive trunk, letting the laughter fall like a wash of red leaves all around us. Scraps and curls of the laughter followed us as we ran. Our breath gave out at the same time our legs did. After we rested against a tree, our heads on crossed forearms, I said, "Let's go home."

Frieda was still angry—fighting, she believed, for her life. "No, we got to get it now."

"We can't go all the way to the lake."

"Yes we can. Come on."

"Mama gone get us."

"No she ain't. Besides, she can't do nothing but whip us."

That was true. She wouldn't kill us, or laugh a terrible laugh at us, or throw a bottle at us.

We walked down tree-lined streets of soft gray houses leaning like tired ladies. . . . The streets changed; houses looked more sturdy, their paint was newer, porch posts straighter, yards deeper. Then came brick houses set well back from the street, fronted by yards edged in shrubbery clipped into smooth cones and balls of velvet green.

The lakefront houses were the loveliest. Garden furniture, ornaments, windows like shiny eyeglasses, and no sign of life. The backyards of these houses fell away in green slopes down to a strip of sand, and then the blue Lake Erie, lapping all the way to Canada. The orange-patched sky of the steel-mill section never reached this part of town. This sky was always blue.

We reached Lake Shore Park, a city park laid out with rosebuds, fountains, bowling greens, picnic tables. It was empty now, but sweetly expectant of clean, white, well-behaved children and parents who would play there above the lake in summer before half-running, half-stumbling down the slope to the welcoming water. Black people were not allowed in the park, and so it filled our dreams.

Right before the entrance to the park was the large white house with the wheelbarrow full of flowers. Short crocus blades sheathed the purple-and-white hearts that so wished to be first they endured the chill and rain of early spring. The walkway was flagged in calculated disorder, hiding the cunning symmetry. Only fear of discovery and the knowledge that we did not belong kept us from loitering. We circled the proud house and went to the back.

There on the tiny railed stoop sat Pecola in a light red sweater and blue cotton dress. A little wagon was parked near her. She seemed glad to see us.

"Hi."

"Hi."

"What you all doing here?" She was smiling, and since it was a rare thing to see on her, I was surprised at the pleasure it gave me.

"We're looking for you."

"Who told you I was here?"

"The Maginot Line."

"Who is that?"

"That big fat lady. She lives over you."

"Oh, you mean Miss Marie. Her name is Miss Marie."

"Well, everybody calls her Miss Maginot Line. Ain't you scared?"

"Scared of what?"

"The Maginot Line."

Pecola looked genuinely puzzled. "What for?"

"Your mama let you go in her house? And eat out of her plates?"

"She don't know I go. Miss Marie is nice. They all nice."

"Oh, yeah," I said, "she tried to kill us."

"Who? Miss Marie? She don't bother nobody."

"Then how come your mama don't let you go in her house if she so nice?"

"I don't know. She say she's bad, but they ain't bad. They give me stuff all the time."

"What stuff?"

"Oh, lots of stuff, pretty dresses, and shoes. I got more shoes than I ever wear. And jewelry and candy and money. They take me to the movies, and once we went to the carnival. China gone take me to Cleveland to see the square, and Poland gone take me to Chicago to see the Loop. We going everywhere together."

"You lying. You don't have no pretty dresses."

"I do, too."

"Oh, come on, Pecola, what you telling us all that junk for?" Frieda asked.

"It ain't junk." Pecola stood up ready to defend her words, when the door opened.

Mrs. Breedlove stuck her head out the door and said, "What's going on out here? Pecola, who are these children?"

"That's Frieda and Claudia, Mrs. Breedlove."

"Whose girls are you?" She came all the way out on the stoop. She looked nicer than I had ever seen her, in her white uniform and her hair in a small pompadour.

"Mrs. MacTeer's girls, ma'am."

"Oh, yes. Live over on Twenty-first Street?"

"Yes, ma'am."

"What are you doing 'way over here?"

"Just walking. We came to see Pecola."

"Well, you better get on back. You can walk with Pecola. Come on in while I get the wash."

We stepped into the kitchen, a large spacious room. Mrs. Breedlove's skin glowed like taffeta in the reflection of white porcelain, white woodwork, polished cabinets, and brilliant copperware. Odors of meat, vegetables, and something freshly baked mixed with a scent of Fels Naphtha.

"I'm gone get the wash. You all stand stock still right there and don't mess up nothing." She disappeared behind a white swinging door, and we could hear the uneven flap of her footsteps as she descended into the basement.

Another door opened, and in walked a little girl, smaller and younger than all of us. She wore a pink sunback dress and pink fluffy bedroom slippers with two bunny ears pointed up from the tips. Her hair was corn yellow and bound in a thick ribbon. When she saw us, fear danced across her face for a second. She looked anxiously around the kitchen.

"Where's Polly?" she asked.

The familiar violence rose in me. Her calling Mrs. Breedlove Polly, when even Pecola called her mother Mrs. Breedlove, seemed reason enough to scratch her.

"She's downstairs," I said.

"Polly!" she called.

"Look," Frieda whispered, "look at that." On the counter near the stove in a silvery pan was a deep-dish berry cobbler. The purple juice bursting here and there through crust. We moved closer.

"It's still hot," Frieda said.

Pecola stretched her hand to touch the pan, lightly, to see if it was hot.

"Polly, come here," the little girl called again.

It may have been nervousness, awkwardness, but the pan tilted under Pecola's fingers and fell to the floor, splattering blackish blueberries everywhere. Most of the juice splashed on Pecola's legs, and the burn must have been painful, for she cried out and began hopping about just as Mrs. Breedlove entered with a tightly packed laundry bag. In one gallop she was on Pecola, and with the back of her hand knocked her to the floor. Pecola slid in the pie juice, one leg folding under her. Mrs. Breedlove yanked her up by the arm, slapped her again, and in a voice thin with anger, abused Pecola directly and Frieda and me by implication.

"Crazy fool . . . my floor, mess . . . look what you . . . work . . . get on out . . . now that . . . crazy . . . my floor, my floor . . . my floor." Her words were hotter and darker than the smoking berries, and we backed away in dread.

The little girl in pink started to cry. Mrs. Breedlove turned to her. "Hush, baby, hush. Come here. Oh, Lord, look at your dress. Don't cry no more. Polly will change it." She went to the sink and turned tap water on a fresh towel. Over her shoulder she spit out words to us like rotten pieces of apple. "Pick up that wash and get on out of here, so I can get this mess cleaned up."

Pecola picked up the laundry bag, heavy with wet clothes, and we stepped hurriedly out the door. As Pecola put the laundry bag in the wagon, we could hear Mrs. Breedlove hushing and soothing the tears of the little pink-and-yellow girl.

"Who were they, Polly?"

"Don't worry none, baby."

"You gonna make another pie?"

" 'Course I will."

"Who were they, Polly?"

"Hush. Don't worry none," she whispered, and the honey in her words complemented the sundown spilling on the lake.

SEEMOTHERMOTHERISVERYNICEMO
THERWILLYOUPLAYWITHJANEMOTH
ERLAUGHSLAUGHMOTHERLAUGHLA

The easiest thing to do would be to build a case out of her foot. That is what she herself did. But to find out the truth about how dreams die, one should never take the word of the dreamer. The end of her lovely beginning was probably the cavity in one of her front teeth. She preferred, however, to think always of her foot. Although she was the ninth of eleven children and lived on a ridge of red Alabama clay seven miles from the nearest road, the complete indifference with which a rusty nail was met when it punched clear through her foot during her second year of life saved Pauline Williams from total anonymity. The wound left her with a crooked, archless foot that flopped when she walked—not a limp that would have eventually twisted her spine, but a way of lifting the bad foot as though she were extracting it from little whirlpools that threatened to pull it under. Slight as it was, this deformity explained for her many things that would have been otherwise incomprehensible: why she alone of all the children had no nickname; why there were no funny jokes and anecdotes about funny things she had done; why no one ever remarked on her food preferences— no saving of the wing or neck for her—no cooking of the peas in a separate pot without rice because she did not like rice; why nobody teased her; why she never felt at home anywhere, or that she belonged anyplace. Her general feeling of separateness and unworthiness she blamed on her foot. Restricted, as a child, to this cocoon of her family's spinning, she cultivated quiet and private pleasures. She liked, most of all, to arrange things. To line things up in rows—jars on shelves at canning, peach pits on the step, sticks, stones, leaves—and the members of her family let these arrangements be. When by some accident somebody scattered her rows, they always stopped to retrieve them for her, and she was never angry, for it gave her a chance to rearrange them again. Whatever portable plurality she found, she organized into neat lines, according to their size, shape, or gradations of color. Just as she would never align a pine needle with the leaf of a cottonwood tree, she would never put the jars of tomatoes next to the green beans. During all of her four years of going to school, she was enchanted by numbers and depressed by words. She missed—without knowing what she missed—paints and crayons.

Near the beginning of World War I, the Williamses discovered, from returning neighbors and kin, the possibility of living better in another place. In shifts, lots, batches, mixed in with other families, they migrated, in six months and four journeys, to Kentucky, where there were mines and millwork.

*"When all us left from down home and was waiting
down by the depot for the truck, it was nighttime. June
bugs was shooting everywhere. They lighted up a tree
leaf, and I seen a streak of green every now and again.
That was the last time I seen real june bugs. These things
up here ain't june bugs. They's something else. Folks here
call them fireflies. Down home they was different. But I
recollect that streak of green. I recollect it well."*

In Kentucky they lived in a real town, ten to fifteen houses
on a single street, with water piped right into the kitchen.
Ada and Fowler Williams found a five-room frame house
for their family. The yard was bounded by a once-white
fence against which Pauline's mother planted flowers and
within which they kept a few chickens. Some of her brothers
joined the Army, one sister died, and two got married,
increasing the living space and giving the entire Kentucky
venture a feel of luxury. The relocation was especially comfortable to Pauline, who was old enough to leave school.
Mrs. Williams got a job cleaning and cooking for a white
minister on the other side of town, and Pauline, now the
oldest girl at home, took over the care of the house. She kept
the fence in repair, pulling the pointed stakes erect, securing
them with bits of wire, collected eggs, swept, cooked,
washed, and minded the two younger children—a pair of
twins called Chicken and Pie, who were still in school. She
was not only good at housekeeping, she enjoyed it. After her
parents left for work and the other children were at school
or in mines, the house was quiet. The stillness and isolation
both calmed and energized her. She could arrange and clean
without interruption until two o'clock, when Chicken and
Pie came home.

When the war ended and the twins were ten years old, they too left school to work. Pauline was fifteen, still keeping house, but with less enthusiasm. Fantasies about men and love and touching were drawing her mind and hands away from her work. Changes in weather began to affect her, as did certain sights and sounds. These feelings translated themselves to her in extreme melancholy. She thought of the death of newborn things, lonely roads, and strangers who appear out of nowhere simply to hold one's hand, woods in which the sun was always setting. In church especially did these dreams grow. The songs caressed her, and while she tried to hold her mind on the wages of sin, her body trembled for redemption, salvation, a mysterious rebirth that would simply happen, with no effort on her part. In none of her fantasies was she ever aggressive; she was usually idling by the river bank, or gathering berries in a field when a someone appeared, with gentle and penetrating eyes, who—with no exchange of words—understood; and before whose glance her foot straightened and her eyes dropped. The someone had no face, no form, no voice, no odor. He was a simple Presence, an all-embracing tenderness with strength and a promise of rest. It did not matter that she had no idea of what to do or say to the Presence—after the wordless knowing and the soundless touching, her dreams disintegrated. But the Presence would know what to do. She had only to lay her head on his chest and he would lead her away to the sea, to the city, to the woods . . . forever.

There was a woman named Ivy who seemed to hold in her mouth all of the sounds of Pauline's soul. Standing a little apart from the choir, Ivy sang the dark sweetness that Pauline could not name; she sang the death-defying death

that Pauline yearned for; she sang of the Stranger who
knew . . .

>Precious Lord take my hand
>Lead me on, let me stand
>I am tired, I am weak, I am worn.
>Through the storms, through the night
>Lead me on to the light
>Take my hand, precious Lord, lead me on.

>When my way grows drear
>Precious Lord linger near,
>When my life is almost gone
>Hear my cry hear my call
>Hold my hand lest I fall
>Take my hand, precious Lord, lead me on.

Thus it was that when the Stranger, the someone, did
appear out of nowhere, Pauline was grateful but not
surprised.

He came, strutting right out of a Kentucky sun on the
hottest day of the year. He came big, he came strong, he
came with yellow eyes, flaring nostrils, and he came with his
own music.

Pauline was leaning idly on the fence, her arms resting
on the crossrail between the pickets. She had just put
down some biscuit dough and was cleaning the flour from
under her nails. Behind her at some distance she heard
whistling. One of these rapid, high-note riffs that black
boys make up as they go while sweeping, shoveling, or just
walking along. A kind of city-street music where laughter
belies anxiety, and joy is as short and straight as the blade

of a pocketknife. She listened carefully to the music and let it pull her lips into a smile. The whistling got louder, and still she did not turn around, for she wanted it to last. While smiling to herself and holding fast to the break in somber thoughts, she felt something tickling her foot. She laughed aloud and turned to see. The whistler was bending down tickling her broken foot and kissing her leg. She could not stop her laughter—not until he looked up at her and she saw the Kentucky sun drenching the yellow, heavy-lidded eyes of Cholly Breedlove.

"When I first seed Cholly, I want you to know it was like all the bits of color from that time down home when all us chil'ren went berry picking after a funeral and I put some in the pocket of my Sunday dress, and they mashed up and stained my hips. My whole dress was messed with purple, and it never did wash out. Not the dress nor me. I could feel that purple deep inside me. And that lemonade Mama used to make when Pap came in out the fields. It be cool and yellowish, with seeds floating near the bottom. And that streak of green them june bugs made on the trees the night we left from down home. All of them colors was in me. Just sitting there. So when Cholly come up and tickled my foot, it was like them berries, that lemonade, them streaks of green the june bugs made, all come together. Cholly was thin then, with real light eyes. He used to whistle, and when I heerd him, shivers come on my skin."

Pauline and Cholly loved each other. He seemed to relish her company and even to enjoy her country ways and lack of knowledge about city things. He talked with her about her foot and asked, when they walked through the town or in the fields, if she were tired. Instead of ignoring her infirmity, pretending it was not there, he made it seem like something special and endearing. For the first time Pauline felt that her bad foot was an asset.

And he did touch her, firmly but gently, just as she had dreamed. But minus the gloom of setting suns and lonely river banks. She was secure and grateful; he was kind and lively. She had not known there was so much laughter in the world.

They agreed to marry and go 'way up north, where Cholly said steel mills were begging for workers. Young, loving, and full of energy, they came to Lorain, Ohio. Cholly found work in the steel mills right away, and Pauline started keeping house.

And then she lost her front tooth. But there must have been a speck, a brown speck easily mistaken for food but which did not leave, which sat on the enamel for months, and grew, until it cut into the surface and then to the brown putty underneath, finally eating away to the root, but avoiding the nerves, so its presence was not noticeable or uncomfortable. Then the weakened roots, having grown accustomed to the poison, responded one day to severe pressure, and the tooth fell free, leaving a ragged stump behind. But even before the little brown speck, there must have been the conditions, the setting that would allow it to exist in the first place.

In that young and growing Ohio town whose side streets, even, were paved with concrete, which sat on the edge of a calm blue lake, which boasted an affinity with Oberlin, the underground railroad station, just thirteen miles away, this

melting pot on the lip of America facing the cold but recep-
tive Canada—What could go wrong?

*"Me and Cholly was getting along good then. We
come up north; supposed to be more jobs and all. We
moved into two rooms up over a furniture store, and I
set about housekeeping. Cholly was working at the steel
plant, and everything was looking good. I don't know
what all happened. Everything changed. It was hard to
get to know folks up here, and I missed my people. I
weren't used to so much white folks. The ones I seed
before was something hateful, but they didn't come
around too much. I mean, we didn't have too much truck
with them. Just now and then in the fields, or at the
commissary. But they want all over us. Up north they
was everywhere—next door, downstairs, all over the
streets—and colored folks few and far between. Northern
colored folk was different too. Dicty-like. No better than
whites for meanness. They could make you feel just as
no-count, 'cept I didn't expect it from them. That was
the lonesomest time of my life. I 'member looking out
them front windows just waiting for Cholly to come
home at three o'clock. I didn't even have a cat to talk
to."*

In her loneliness, she turned to her husband for reassur-
ance, entertainment, for things to fill the vacant places.
Housework was not enough; there were only two rooms,
and no yard to keep or move about in. The women in the
town wore high-heeled shoes, and when Pauline tried to
wear them, they aggravated her shuffle into a pronounced

limp. Cholly was kindness still, but began to resist her total dependence on him. They were beginning to have less and less to say to each other. He had no problem finding other people and other things to occupy him—men were always climbing the stairs asking for him, and he was happy to accompany them, leaving her alone.

Pauline felt uncomfortable with the few black women she met. They were amused by her because she did not straighten her hair. When she tried to make up her face as they did, it came off rather badly. Their goading glances and private snickers at her way of talking (saying "chil'ren") and dressing developed in her a desire for new clothes. When Cholly began to quarrel about the money she wanted, she decided to go to work. Taking jobs as a day worker helped with the clothes, and even a few things for the apartment, but it did not help with Cholly. He was not pleased with her purchases and began to tell her so. Their marriage was shredded with quarrels. She was still no more than a girl, and still waiting for that plateau of happiness, that hand of a precious Lord who, when her way grew drear, would always linger near. Only now she had a clearer idea of what drear meant. Money became the focus of all their discussions, hers for clothes, his for drink. The sad thing was that Pauline did not really care for clothes and makeup. She merely wanted other women to cast favorable glances her way.

After several months of doing day work, she took a steady job in the home of a family of slender means and nervous, pretentious ways.

"Cholly commenced to getting meaner and meaner and wanted to fight me all of the time. I give him as good as

I got. Had to. Look like working for that woman and
fighting Cholly was all I did. Tiresome. But I holt on to
my jobs, even though working for that woman was more
than a notion. It wasn't so much her meanness as just
simpleminded. Her whole family was. Couldn't get along
with one another worth nothing. You'd think with a
pretty house like that and all the money they could holt
on to, they would enjoy one another. She haul off and
cry over the leastest thing. If one of her friends cut her
short on the telephone, she'd go to crying. She should of
been glad she had a telephone. I ain't got one yet. I
recollect oncet how her baby brother who she put
through dentistry school didn't invite them to some big
party he throwed. They was a big to-do about that.
Everybody stayed on the telephone for days. Fussing and
carrying on. She asked me, 'Pauline, what would you do
if your own brother had a party and didn't invite you?' I
said ifn I really wanted to go to that party, I reckoned I'd
go anyhow. Never mind what he want. She just sucked
her teeth a little and made out like what I said was
dumb. All the while I was thinking how dumb she was.
Whoever told her that her brother was her friend? Folks
can't like folks just 'cause they has the same mama. I
tried to like that woman myself. She was good about
giving me stuff, but I just couldn't like her. Soon as I
worked up a good feeling on her account, she'd do
something ignorant and start in to telling me how to
clean and do. If I left her on her own, she'd drown in
dirt. I didn't have to pick up after Chicken and Pie the
way I had to pick up after them. None of them knew so
much as how to wipe their behinds. I know, 'cause I did
the washing. And couldn't pee proper to save their lives.

*Her husband ain't hit the bowl yet. Nasty white folks is
about the nastiest things they is. But I would have stayed
on 'cepting for Cholly come over by where I was
working and cut up so. He come there drunk wanting
some money. When that white woman see him, she
turned red. She tried to act strong-like, but she was
scared bad. Anyway, she told Cholly to get out or she
would call the police. He cussed her and started pulling
on me. I would of gone upside his head, but I don't want
no dealings with the police. So I taken my things and left.
I tried to get back, but she didn't want me no more if I
was going to stay with Cholly. She said she would let me
stay if I left him. I thought about that. But later on it
didn't seem none too bright for a black woman to leave a
black man for a white woman. She didn't never give me
the eleven dollars she owed me, neither. That hurt bad.
The gas man had cut the gas off, and I couldn't cook
none. I really begged that woman for my money. I went
to see her. She was mad as a wet hen. Kept on telling me
I owed her for uniforms and some old broken-down bed
she give me. I didn't know if I owed her or not, but I
needed my money. She wouldn't let up none, neither,
even when I give her my word that Cholly wouldn't
come back there no more. Then I got so desperate I
asked her if she would loan it to me. She was quiet for a
spell, and then she told me I shouldn't let a man take
advantage over me. That I should have more respect, and
it was my husband's duty to pay the bills, and if he
couldn't, I should leave and get alimony. All such simple
stuff. What was he gone give me alimony on? I seen she
didn't understand that all I needed from her was my*

eleven dollars to pay the gas man so I could cook. She
couldn't get that one thing through her thick head. 'Are
you going to leave him, Pauline?' she kept on saying. I
thought she'd give me my money if I said I would, so I
said 'Yes, ma'am.' 'All right,' she said. 'You leave him,
and then come back to work, and we'll let bygones be
bygones.' 'Can I have my money today?' I said. 'No' she
said. 'Only when you leave him. I'm only thinking of you
and your future. What good is he, Pauline, what good is
he to you?' How you going to answer a woman like that,
who don't know what good a man is, and say out of one
side of her mouth she's thinking of your future but won't
give you your own money so you can buy you something
besides baloney to eat? So I said, 'No good, ma'am. He
ain't no good to me. But just the same, I think I'd best
stay on.' She got up, and I left. When I got outside, I felt
pains in my crotch, I had held my legs together so tight
trying to make that woman understand. But I reckon
now she couldn't understand. She married a man with a
slash in his face instead of a mouth. So how could she
understand?"

One winter Pauline discovered she was pregnant. When
she told Cholly, he surprised her by being pleased. He began
to drink less and come home more often. They eased back
into a relationship more like the early days of their marriage, when he asked if she were tired or wanted him to
bring her something from the store. In this state of ease,
Pauline stopped doing day work and returned to her own
housekeeping. But the loneliness in those two rooms had not
gone away. When the winter sun hit the peeling green paint

of the kitchen chairs, when the smoked hocks were boiling in the pot, when all she could hear was the truck delivering furniture downstairs, she thought about back home, about how she had been all alone most of the time then too, but that this lonesomeness was different. Then she stopped staring at the green chairs, at the delivery truck; she went to the movies instead. There in the dark her memory was refreshed, and she succumbed to her earlier dreams. Along with the idea of romantic love, she was introduced to another—physical beauty. Probably the most destructive ideas in the history of human thought. Both originated in envy, thrived in insecurity, and ended in disillusion. In equating physical beauty with virtue, she stripped her mind, bound it, and collected self-contempt by the heap. She forgot lust and simple caring for. She regarded love as possessive mating, and romance as the goal of the spirit. It would be for her a well-spring from which she would draw the most destructive emotions, deceiving the lover and seeking to imprison the beloved, curtailing freedom in every way.

She was never able, after her education in the movies, to look at a face and not assign it some category in the scale of absolute beauty, and the scale was one she absorbed in full from the silver screen. There at last were the darkened woods, the lonely roads, the river banks, the gentle knowing eyes. There the flawed became whole, the blind sighted, and the lame and halt threw away their crutches. There death was dead, and people made every gesture in a cloud of music. There the black-and-white images came together, making a magnificent whole—all projected through the ray of light from above and behind.

It was really a simple pleasure, but she learned all there was to love and all there was to hate.

"The onliest time I be happy seem like was when I was in the picture show. Every time I got, I went. I'd go early, before the show started. They'd cut off the lights, and everything be black. Then the screen would light up, and I'd move right on in them pictures. White men taking such good care of they women, and they all dressed up in big clean houses with the bathtubs right in the same room with the toilet. Them pictures gave me a lot of pleasure, but it made coming home hard, and looking at Cholly hard. I don't know. I 'member one time I went to see Clark Gable and Jean Harlow. I fixed my hair up like I'd seen hers on a magazine. A part on the side, with one little curl on my forehead. It looked just like her. Well, almost just like. Anyway, I sat in that show with my hair done up that way and had a good time. I thought I'd see it through to the end again, and I got up to get me some candy. I was sitting back in my seat, and I taken a big bite of that candy, and it pulled a tooth right out of my mouth. I could of cried. I had good teeth, not a rotten one in my head. I don't believe I ever did get over that. There I was, five months pregnant, trying to look like Jean Harlow, and a front tooth gone. Everything went then. Look like I just didn't care no more after that. I let my hair go back, plaited it up, and settled down to just being ugly. I still went to the pictures, though, but the meanness got worse. I wanted my tooth back. Cholly poked fun at me, and we started fighting again. I tried to kill him. He didn't hit me too hard, 'cause I were pregnant I guess, but the fights, once they got started up again, kept up. He begin to make me madder than anything I knowed, and I couldn't keep my hands off him. Well, I had that baby—a boy—and after *that got pregnant again with another one. But it weren't like I thought it was gone be. I loved them and all, I guess, but maybe it was having no money, or maybe it was Cholly, but they sure worried the life out of me. Sometimes I'd catch myself hollering at them and beating them, and I'd feel sorry for them, but I couldn't seem to stop. When I had the second one, a girl, I 'member I said I'd love it no matter what it looked like. She looked like a black ball of hair. I don't recollect trying to get pregnant that first time. But that second time, I actually tried to get pregnant. Maybe 'cause I'd had one already and wasn't scairt to do it. Anyway, I felt good, and wasn't thinking on the carrying, just the baby itself. I used to talk to it whilst it be still in the womb. Like good friends we was. You know. I be hanging wash and I knowed lifting weren't good for it. I'd say to it holt on now I gone hang up these few rags, don't get froggy; it be over soon. It wouldn't leap or nothing. Or I be mixing something in a bowl for the other chile and I'd talk to it then too. You know, just friendly talk. On up til the end I felted good about that baby. I went to the hospital when my time come. So I could be easeful. I didn't want to have it at home like I done with the boy. They put me in a big room with a whole mess of women. The pains was coming, but not too bad. A little old doctor come to examine me. He had all sorts of stuff. He gloved his hand and put some kind of jelly on it and rammed it up between my legs. When he left off, some more doctors come. One old one and some young ones. The old one was learning the young ones about babies. Showing them how to do. When he got to me he said now these here women you don't have any trouble with. They deliver*

right away and with no pain. Just like horses. The young
ones smiled a little. They looked at my stomach and
between my legs. They never said nothing to me. Only
one looked at me. Looked at my face, I mean. I looked
right back at him. He dropped his eyes and turned red.
He knowed, I reckon, that maybe I weren't no horse
foaling. But them others. They didn't know. They went
on. I seed them talking to them white women: 'How you
feel? Gonna have twins?' Just shucking them, of course,
but nice talk. Nice friendly talk. I got edgy, and when
them pains got harder, I was glad. Glad to have
something else to think about. I moaned something
awful. The pains wasn't as bad as I let on, but I had to
let them people know having a baby was more than a
bowel movement. I hurt just like them white women. Just
'cause I wasn't hooping and hollering before didn't mean
I wasn't feeling pain. What'd they think? That just 'cause
I knowed how to have a baby with no fuss that my
behind wasn't pulling and aching like theirs? Besides, that
doctor don't know what he talking about. He must never
seed no mare foal. Who say they don't have no pain? Just
'cause she don't cry? 'Cause she can't say it, they think it
ain't there? If they looks in her eyes and see them
eyeballs lolling back, see the sorrowful look, they'd
know. Anyways, the baby come. Big old healthy thing.
She looked different from what I thought. Reckon I
talked to it so much before I conjured up a mind's eye
view of it. So when I seed it, it was like looking at a
picture of your mama when she was a girl. You knows
who she is, but she don't look the same. They give her to
me for a nursing, and she liked to pull my nipple off
right away. She caught on fast. Not like Sammy, he was

the hardest child to feed. But Pecola look like she
knowed right off what to do. A right smart baby she
was. I used to like to watch her. You know they makes
them greedy sounds. Eyes all soft and wet. A cross
between a puppy and a dying man. But I knowed she was
ugly. Head full of pretty hair, but Lord she was ugly."

When Sammy and Pecola were still young Pauline had to
go back to work. She was older now, with no time for
dreams and movies. It was time to put all of the pieces
together, make coherence where before there had been
none. The children gave her this need; she herself was no
longer a child. So she became, and her process of becoming
was like most of ours: she developed a hatred for things that
mystified or obstructed her; acquired virtues that were easy
to maintain; assigned herself a role in the scheme of things;
and harked back to simpler times for gratification.

She took on the full responsibility and recognition of
breadwinner and returned to church. First, however, she
moved out of the two rooms into a spacious first floor of a
building that had been built as a store. She came into her
own with the women who had despised her, by being more
moral than they; she avenged herself on Cholly by forcing
him to indulge in the weaknesses she despised. She joined a
church where shouting was frowned upon, served on Stew-
ardess Board No. 3, and became a member of Ladies Circle
No. 1. At prayer meeting she moaned and sighed over
Cholly's ways, and hoped God would help her keep the
children from the sins of the father. She stopped saying
"chil'ren" and said "childring" instead. She let another
tooth fall, and was outraged by painted ladies who thought
only of clothes and men. Holding Cholly as a model of sin

and failure, she bore him like a crown of thorns, and her children like a cross.

It was her good fortune to find a permanent job in the home of a well-to-do family whose members were affectionate, appreciative, and generous. She looked at their houses, smelled their linen, touched their silk draperies, and loved all of it. The child's pink nightie, the stacks of white pillow slips edged with embroidery, the sheets with top hems picked out with blue cornflowers. She became what is known as an ideal servant, for such a role filled practically all of her needs. When she bathed the little Fisher girl, it was in a porcelain tub with silvery taps running infinite quantities of hot, clear water. She dried her in fluffy white towels and put her in cuddly night clothes. Then she brushed the yellow hair, enjoying the roll and slip of it between her fingers. No zinc tub, no buckets of stove-heated water, no flaky, stiff, grayish towels washed in a kitchen sink, dried in a dusty backyard, no tangled black puffs of rough wool to comb. Soon she stopped trying to keep her own house. The things she could afford to buy did not last, had no beauty or style, and were absorbed by the dingy storefront. More and more she neglected her house, her children, her man—they were like the afterthoughts one has just before sleep, the early-morning and late-evening edges of her day, the dark edges that made the daily life with the Fishers lighter, more delicate, more lovely. Here she could arrange things, clean things, line things up in neat rows. Here her foot flopped around on deep pile carpets, and there was no uneven sound. Here she found beauty, order, cleanliness, and praise. Mr. Fisher said, "I would rather sell her blueberry cobblers than real estate." She reigned over cupboards stacked high with food that would not be eaten for weeks, even months; she was queen of canned vegetables bought by the case, special fondants and ribbon candy curled up in tiny silver dishes. The creditors and service people who humiliated her when she went to them on her own behalf respected her, were even intimidated by her, when she spoke for the Fishers. She refused beef slightly dark or with edges not properly trimmed. The slightly reeking fish that she accepted for her own family she would all but throw in the fish man's face if he sent it to the Fisher house. Power, praise, and luxury were hers in this household. They even gave her what she had never had—a nickname—Polly. It was her pleasure to stand in her kitchen at the end of a day and survey her handiwork. Knowing there were soap bars by the dozen, bacon by the rasher, and reveling in her shiny pots and pans and polished floors. Hearing, "We'll never let her go. We could never find anybody like Polly. She will *not* leave the kitchen until everything is in order. Really, she is the ideal servant."

Pauline kept this order, this beauty, for herself, a private world, and never introduced it into her storefront, or to her children. Them she bent toward respectability, and in so doing taught them fear: fear of being clumsy, fear of being like their father, fear of not being loved by God, fear of madness like Cholly's mother's. Into her son she beat a loud desire to run away, and into her daughter she beat a fear of growing up, fear of other people, fear of life.

All the meaningfulness of her life was in her work. For her virtues were intact. She was an active church woman, did not drink, smoke, or carouse, defended herself mightily against Cholly, rose above him in every way, and felt she was fulfilling a mother's role conscientiously when she pointed out their father's faults to keep them from having them, or punished them when they showed any slovenliness, no matter how slight, when she worked twelve to sixteen hours a day to support them. And the world itself agreed with her.

It was only sometimes, sometimes, and then rarely, that she thought about the old days, or what her life had turned to. They were musings, idle thoughts, full sometimes of the old dreaminess, but not the kind of thing she cared to dwell on.

"I started to leave him once, but something came up. Once, after he tried to set the house on fire, I was all set in my mind to go. I can't even 'member now what held me. He sure ain't give me much of a life. But it wasn't all bad. Sometimes things wasn't all bad. He used to come easing into bed sometimes, not too drunk. I make out like I'm asleep, 'cause it's late, and he taken three dollars out of my pocketbook that morning or something. I hear him breathing, but I don't look around. I can see in my mind's eye his black arms thrown back behind his head, the muscles like great big peach stones sanded down, with veins running like little swollen rivers down his arms. Without touching him I be feeling those ridges on the tips of my fingers. I sees the palms of his hands calloused to granite, and the long fingers curled up and still. I think about the thick, knotty hair on his chest, and the two big swells his breast muscles make. I want to rub my face hard in his chest and feel the hair cut my skin. I know just where the hair growth slacks out—just above his navel—and how it picks up again and spreads out. Maybe he'll shift a little, and his leg will touch me, or I feel his flank just graze my behind. I don't move even yet.

Then he lift his head, turn over, and put his hand on my waist. If I don't move, he'll move his hand over to pull and knead my stomach. Soft and slow-like. I still don't move, because I don't want him to stop. I want to pretend sleep and have him keep on rubbing my stomach. Then he will lean his head down and bite my tit. Then I don't want him to rub my stomach anymore. I want him to put his hand between my legs. I pretend to wake up, and turn to him, but not opening my legs. I want him to open them for me. He does, and I be soft and wet where his fingers are strong and hard. I be softer than I ever been before. All my strength in his hand. My brain curls up like wilted leaves. A funny, empty feeling is in my hands. I want to grab holt of something, so I hold his head. His mouth is under my chin. Then I don't want his hand between my legs no more, because I think I am softening away. I stretch my legs open, and he is on top of me. Too heavy to hold, and too light not to. He puts his thing in me. In me. In me. I wrap my feet around his back so he can't get away. His face is next to mine. The bed springs sounds like them crickets used to back home. He puts his fingers in mine, and we stretches our arms outwise like Jesus on the cross. I hold on tight. My fingers and my feet hold on tight, because everything else is going, going. I know he wants me to come first. But I can't. Not until he does. Not until I feel him loving me. Just me. Sinking into me. Not until I know that my flesh is all that be on his mind. That he couldn't stop if he had to. That he would die rather than take his thing out of me. Of me. Not until he has let go of all he has, and give it to me. To me. To me. When he does, I feel a power. I be strong, I be pretty, I be young. And then I wait. He

shivers and tosses his head. Now I be strong enough,
pretty enough, and young enough to let him make me
come. I take my fingers out of his and put my hands on
his behind. My legs drop back onto the bed. I don't make
no noise, because the chil'ren might hear. I begin to feel
those little bits of color floating up into me— deep in me.
That streak of green from the june-bug light, the purple
from the berries trickling along my thighs, Mama's
lemonade yellow runs sweet in me. Then I feel like I'm
laughing between my legs, and the laughing gets all
mixed up with the colors, and I'm afraid I'll come, and
afraid I won't. But I know I will. And I do. And it be
rainbow all inside. And it lasts and lasts and lasts. I want
to thank him, but don't know how, so I pat him like you
do a baby. He asks me if I'm all right. I say yes. He gets
off me and lies down to sleep. I want to say something,
but I don't. I don't want to take my mind offen the
rainbow. I should get up and go to the toilet, but I don't.
Besides, Cholly is asleep with his leg throwed over me. I
can't move and don't want to.

"But it ain't like that anymore. Most times he's
thrashing away inside me before I'm woke, and through
when I am. The rest of the time I can't even be next to
his stinking drunk self. But I don't care 'bout it no more.
My Maker will take care of me. I know He will. I know
He will. Besides, it don't make no difference about this
old earth. There is sure to be a glory. Only thing I miss
sometimes is that rainbow. But like I say, I don't recollect
it much anymore."

SEEFATHERHEISBIGANDSTRONGFATH
ERWILLYOUPLAYWITHJANEFATHER
ISSMILINGSMILEFATHERSMILESMILE

When Cholly was four days old, his mother wrapped him in two blankets and one newspaper and placed him on a junk heap by the railroad. His Great Aunt Jimmy, who had seen her niece carrying a bundle out of the back door, rescued him. She beat his mother with a razor strap and wouldn't let her near the baby after that. Aunt Jimmy raised Cholly herself, but took delight sometimes in telling him of how she had saved him. He gathered from her that his mother wasn't right in the head. But he never had a chance to find out, because she ran away shortly after the razor strap, and no one had heard of her since.

Cholly was grateful for having been saved. Except sometimes. Sometimes when he watched Aunt Jimmy eating collards with her fingers, sucking her four gold teeth, or smelled her when she wore the asafetida bag around her neck, or when she made him sleep with her for warmth in winter and he could see her old, wrinkled breasts sagging in her nightgown—then he wondered whether it would have been just as well to have died there. Down in the rim of a tire under a soft black Georgia sky.

He had four years of school before he got courage enough to ask his aunt who and where his father was.

"That Fuller boy, I believe it was," his aunt said. "He was hanging around then, but he taken off pretty quick before you was born. I think he gone to Macon. Him or his brother. Maybe both. I hear old man Fuller say something 'bout it once."

"What name he have?" asked Cholly.

"Fuller, Foolish."

"I mean what his given name?"

"Oh." She closed her eyes to think, and sighed. "Can't recollect nothing no more. Sam, was it? Yeh. Samuel. No. No, it wasn't. It was Samson. Samson Fuller."

"How come you all didn't name me Samson?" Cholly's voice was low.

"What for? He wasn't nowhere around when you was born. Your mama didn't name you nothing. The nine days wasn't up before she throwed you on the junk heap. When I got you I named you myself on the ninth day. You named after my dead brother. Charles Breedlove. A good man. Ain't no Samson never come to no good end."

Cholly didn't ask anything else.

Two years later he quit school to take a job at Tyson's Feed and Grain Store. He swept up, ran errands, weighed bags, and lifted them onto the drays. Sometimes they let him ride with the drayman. A nice old man called Blue Jack. Blue used to tell him old-timey stories about how it was when the Emancipation Proclamation came. How the black people hollered, cried, and sang. And ghost stories about how a white man cut off his wife's head and buried her in the swamp, and the headless body came out at night and went stumbling around the yard, knocking over stuff because it couldn't see, and crying all the time for a comb. They talked about the women Blue had had, and the fights he'd been in when he was younger, about how he talked his way out of getting lynched once, and how others hadn't.

Cholly loved Blue. Long after he was a man, he remembered the good times they had had. How on a July 4 at a church picnic a family was about to break open a watermelon. Several children were standing around watching. Blue was hovering about on the periphery of the circle—a faint smile of anticipation softening his face. The father of the family lifted the melon high over his head—his big arms looked taller than the trees to Cholly, and the melon blotted out the sun. Tall, head forward, eyes fastened on a rock, his arms higher than the pines, his hands holding a melon bigger than the sun, he paused an instant to get his bearing and secure his aim. Watching the figure etched against the bright blue sky, Cholly felt goose pimples popping along his arms and neck. He wondered if God looked like that. No. God was a nice old white man, with long white hair, flowing white beard, and little blue eyes that looked sad when people died and mean when they were bad. It must be the devil who looks like that—holding the world in his hands, ready to dash it to the ground and spill the red guts so niggers could eat the sweet, warm insides. If the devil did look like that, Cholly preferred him. He never felt anything thinking about God, but just the idea of the devil excited him. And now the strong, black devil was blotting out the sun and getting ready to split open the world.

Far away somebody was playing a mouth organ; the

music slithered over the cane fields and into the pine grove; it spiraled around the tree trunks and mixed itself with the pine scent, so Cholly couldn't tell the difference between the sound and the odor that hung about the heads of the people.

The man swung the melon down to the edge of a rock. A soft cry of disappointment accompanied the sound of smashed rind. The break was a bad one. The melon was jagged, and hunks of rind and red meat scattered on the grass.

Blue jumped. "Aw—awww," he moaned, "dere go da heart." His voice was both sad and pleased. Everybody looked to see the big red chunk from the very center of the melon, free of rind and sparse of seed, which had rolled a little distance from Blue's feet. He stooped to pick it up. Blood red, its planes dull and blunted with sweetness, its edges rigid with juice. Too obvious, almost obscene, in the joy it promised.

"Go 'head, Blue," the father laughed. "You can have it."

Blue smiled and walked away. Little children scrambled for the pieces on the ground. Women picked out the seeds for the smallest ones and broke off little bits of the meat for themselves. Blue's eye caught Cholly's. He motioned to him. "Come on, boy. Le's you and me eat the heart."

Together the old man and the boy sat on the grass and shared the heart of the watermelon. The nasty-sweet guts of the earth.

It was in the spring, a very chilly spring, that Aunt Jimmy died of peach cobbler. She went to a camp meeting that took place after a rainstorm, and the damp wood of the benches was bad for her. For four or five days afterward, she felt poorly. Friends came to see about her. Some made camomile tea; others rubbed her with liniment. Miss Alice, her closest friend, read the Bible to her. Still she was declining. Advice was prolific, if contradictory.

"Don't eat no whites of eggs."

"Drink new milk."

"Chew on this root."

Aunt Jimmy ignored all but Miss Alice's Bible reading. She nodded in drowsy appreciation as the words from First Corinthians droned over her. Sweet amens fell from her lips as she was chastised for all her sins. But her body would not respond.

Finally it was decided to fetch M'Dear. M'Dear was a quiet woman who lived in a shack near the woods. She was a competent midwife and decisive diagnostician. Few could remember when M'Dear was not around. In any illness that could not be handled by ordinary means—known cures, intuition, or endurance—the word was always, "Fetch M'Dear."

When she arrived at Aunt Jimmy's house, Cholly was amazed at the sight of her. He had always pictured her as shriveled and hunched over, for he knew she was very, very old. But M'Dear loomed taller than the preacher who accompanied her. She must have been over six feet tall. Four big white knots of hair gave power and authority to her soft black face. Standing straight as a poker, she seemed to need her hickory stick not for support but for communication. She tapped it lightly on the floor as she looked down at Aunt Jimmy's wrinkled face. She stroked the knob with the thumb of her right hand while she ran her left one over Aunt Jimmy's body. The backs of her long fingers she placed on the patient's cheek, then placed her palm on the forehead. She ran her fingers through the sick woman's hair, lightly scratching the scalp, and then looking at what the finger-nails revealed. She lifted Aunt Jimmy's hand and looked closely at it—fingernails, back skin, the flesh of the palm she pressed with three fingertips. Later she put her ear on Aunt Jimmy's chest and stomach to listen. At M'Dear's request, the women pulled the slop jar from under the bed to show the stools. M'Dear tapped her stick while looking at them.

"Bury the slop jar and everything in it," she said to the women. To Aunt Jimmy she said, "You done caught cold in your womb. Drink pot liquor and nothing else."

"Will it pass?" asked Aunt Jimmy. "Is I'm gone be all right?"

"I reckon."

M'Dear turned and left the room. The preacher put her in his buggy to take her home.

That evening the women brought bowls of pot liquor from black-eyed peas, from mustards, from cabbage, from kale, from collards, from turnips, from beets, from green beans. Even the juice from a boiling hog jowl.

Two evenings later Aunt Jimmy had gained much strength. When Miss Alice and Mrs. Gaines stopped in to check on her, they remarked on her improvement. The three women sat talking about various miseries they had had, their cure or abatement, what had helped. Over and over again they returned to Aunt Jimmy's condition. Repeating its cause, what could have been done to prevent the misery from taking hold, and M'Dear's infallibility. Their voices blended into a threnody of nostalgia about pain. Rising and falling, complex in harmony, uncertain in pitch, but constant in the recitative of pain. They hugged the memories of illnesses to their bosoms. They licked their lips and clucked their tongues in fond remembrance of pains they had endured—childbirth, rheumatism, croup, sprains, backaches, piles. All of the bruises they had collected from moving about the earth—harvesting, cleaning, hoisting, pitching, stooping, kneeling, picking—always with young ones underfoot.

But they had been young once. The odor of their armpits and haunches had mingled into a lovely musk; their eyes had been furtive, their lips relaxed, and the delicate turn of their heads on those slim black necks had been like nothing other than a doe's. Their laughter had been more touch than sound.

Then they had grown. Edging into life from the back door. Becoming. Everybody in the world was in a position to give them orders. White women said, "Do this." White children said, "Give me that." White men said, "Come here." Black men said, "Lay down." The only people they need not take orders from were black children and each other. But they took all of that and re-created it in their own image. They ran the houses of white people, and knew it. When white men beat their men, they cleaned up the blood and went home to receive abuse from the victim. They beat their children with one hand and stole for them with the other. The hands that felled trees also cut umbilical cords; the hands that wrung the necks of chickens and butchered hogs also nudged African violets into bloom; the arms that loaded sheaves, bales, and sacks rocked babies into sleep. They patted biscuits into flaky ovals of innocence—and shrouded the dead. They plowed all day and came home to nestle like plums under the limbs of their men. The legs that straddled a mule's back were the same ones that straddled their men's hips. And the difference was all the difference there was.

Then they were old. Their bodies honed, their odor sour. Squatting in a cane field, stooping in a cotton field, kneeling by a river bank, they had carried a world on their heads. They had given over the lives of their own children and tendered their grandchildren. With relief they wrapped their heads in rags, and their breasts in flannel; eased their feet into felt. They were through with lust and lactation, beyond tears and terror. They alone could walk the roads of Mississippi, the lanes of Georgia, the fields of Alabama unmolested. They were old enough to be irritable when and where they chose, tired enough to look forward to death, disinterested enough to accept the idea of pain while ignoring the presence of pain. They were, in fact and at last, free. And the lives of these old black women were synthesized in their eyes—a purée of tragedy and humor, wickedness and serenity, truth and fantasy.

They chattered far into the night. Cholly listened and grew sleepy. The lullaby of grief enveloped him, rocked him, and at last numbed him. In his sleep the foul odor of an old woman's stools turned into the healthy smell of horse shit, and the voices of the three women were muted into the pleasant notes of a mouth organ. He was aware, in his sleep, of being curled up in a chair, his hands tucked between his thighs. In a dream his penis changed into a long hickory stick, and the hands caressing it were the hands of M'Dear.

On a wet Saturday night, before Aunt Jimmy felt strong enough to get out of the bed, Essie Foster brought her a peach cobbler. The old lady ate a piece, and the next morning when Cholly went to empty the slop jar, she was dead. Her mouth was a slackened O, and her hands, those long fingers with a man's hard nails, having done their laying by, could now be dainty on the sheet. One open eye looked at

him as if to say, "Mind how you take holt of that jar, boy."
Cholly stared back, unable to move, until a fly settled at the
corner of her mouth. He fanned it away angrily, looked
back at the eye, and did its bidding.

Aunt Jimmy's funeral was the first Cholly had ever at-
tended. As a member of the family, one of the bereaved, he
was the object of a great deal of attention. The ladies had
cleaned the house, aired everything out, notified everybody,
and stitched together what looked like a white wedding
dress for Aunt Jimmy, a maiden lady, to wear when she met
Jesus. They even produced a dark suit, white shirt, and tie
for Cholly. The husband of one of them cut his hair. He was
enclosed in fastidious tenderness. Nobody talked to him;
that is, they treated him like the child he was, never engag-
ing him in serious conversation; but they anticipated wishes
he never had: meals appeared, hot water for the wooden
tub, clothes laid out. At the wake he was allowed to fall
asleep, and arms carried him to bed. Only on the third day
after the death—the day of the funeral—did he have to
share the spotlight. Aunt Jimmy's people came from nearby
towns and farms. Her brother O. V., his children and wife,
and lots of cousins. But Cholly was still the major figure,
because he was "Jimmy's boy, the last thing she loved," and
"the one who found her." The solicitude of the women, the
head pats of the men, pleased Cholly, and the creamy conversations fascinated him.

"What'd she die from?"

"Essie's pie."

"Don't say?"

"Uh-huh. She was doing fine, I saw her the very day
before. Said she wanted me to bring her some black thread

to patch some things for the boy. I should of known just from her wanting black thread that was a sign."

"Sure was."

"Just like Emma. 'Member? She kept asking for thread. Dropped dead that very evening."

"Yeah. Well, she was determined to have it. Kept on reminding me. I told her I had some to home, but naw, she wanted it new. So I sent Li'l June to get some that very morning when she was laying dead. I was just fixing to bring it over, 'long with a piece of sweet bread. You know how she craved my sweet bread."

"Sure did. Always bragged on it. She was a good friend to you."

"I believe it. Well, I had no more got my clothes on when Sally bust in the door hollering about how Cholly here had been over to Miss Alice saying she was dead. You could have knocked me over, I tell you."

"Guess Essie feels mighty bad."

"Oh, Lord, yes. But I told her the Lord giveth and the Lord taketh away. Wasn't her fault none. She makes good peach pies. But she bound to believe it was the pie did it, and I 'spect she right."

"Well, she shouldn't worry herself none 'bout that. She was just doing what we all would of done."

"Yeah. 'Cause I was sure wrapping up that sweet bread, and that could of done it too."

"I doubts that. Sweet bread is pure. But a pie is the worse thing to give anybody ailing. I'm surprised Jimmy didn't know better."

"If she did, she wouldn't let on. She would have tried to please. You know how she was. So good."

"I'll say. Did she leave anything?"

"Not even a pocket handkerchief. The house belongs to some white folks in Clarksville."

"Oh, yeah? I thought she owned it."

"May have at one time. But not no more. I hear the insurance folks been down talking to her brother."

"How much do it come to?"

"Eighty-five dollars, I hear."

"That all?"

"Can she get in the ground on that?"

"Don't see how. When my daddy died last year this April it costed one hundred and fifty dollars. 'Course, we had to have everything just so. Now Jimmy's people may all have to chip in. That undertaker that lays out black folks ain't none too cheap."

"Seems a shame. She been paying on that insurance all her life."

"Don't I know?"

"Well, what about the boy? What he gone do?"

"Well, caint nobody find that mama, so Jimmy's brother gone take him back to his place. They say he got a nice place. Inside toilet and everything."

"That's nice. He seems like a good Christian man. And the boy need a man's hand."

"What time's the funeral?"

"Two clock. She ought to be in the ground by four."

"Where's the banquet? I heard Essie wanted it at her house."

"Naw, it's at Jimmy's. Her brother wanted it so."

"Well, it will be a big one. Everybody liked old Jimmy. Sure will miss her in the pew."

The funeral banquet was a peal of joy after the thunderous beauty of the funeral. It was like a street tragedy with spontaneity tucked softly into the corners of a highly formal structure. The deceased was the tragic hero, the survivors the innocent victims; there was the omnipresence of the deity, strophe and antistrophe of the chorus of mourners led by the preacher. There was grief over the waste of life, the stunned wonder at the ways of God, and the restoration of order in nature at the graveyard.

Thus the banquet was the exultation, the harmony, the acceptance of physical frailty, joy in the termination of misery. Laughter, relief, a steep hunger for food.

Cholly had not yet fully realized his aunt was dead. Everything was so interesting. Even at the graveyard he felt nothing but curiosity, and when his turn had come to view the body at the church, he had put his hand out to touch the corpse to see if it were really ice cold like everybody said. But he drew his hand back quickly. Aunt Jimmy looked so private, and it seemed wrong somehow to disturb that privacy. He had trudged back to his pew dry-eyed amid tearful shrieks and shouts of others, wondering if he should try to cry.

Back in his house, he was free to join in the gaiety and enjoy what he really felt—a kind of carnival spirit. He ate greedily and felt good enough to try to get to know his cousins. There was some question, according to the adults, as to whether they were his real cousins or not, since Jimmy's brother O. V. was only a half-brother, and Cholly's mother had been the daughter of Jimmy's sister, but that sister was from the second marriage of Jimmy's father, and O. V. was from the first marriage.

One of these cousins interested Cholly in particular. He was about fifteen or sixteen years old. Cholly went outside and found the boy standing with some others near the tub where Aunt Jimmy used to boil her clothes.

He ventured a tentative "Hey." They responded with another. The fifteen-year-old named Jake offered Cholly a rolled-up cigarette. Cholly took it, but when he held the cigarette at arm's length and stuck the tip of it into the match flame, instead of putting it in his mouth and drawing on it, they laughed at him. Shamefaced, he threw the cigarette down. He felt it important to do something to reinstate himself with Jake. So when he asked Cholly if he knew any girls, Cholly said, "Sure."

All the girls Cholly knew were at the banquet, and he pointed to a cluster of them standing, hanging, draping on the back porch. Darlene too. Cholly hoped Jake wouldn't pick her.

"Let's get some and walk around," said Jake.

The two boys sauntered over to the porch. Cholly didn't know how to begin. Jake wrapped his legs around the rickety porch rail and just sat there staring off into space as though he had no interest in them at all. He was letting them look him over, and guardedly evaluating them in return.

The girls pretended they didn't see the boys and kept on chattering. Soon their talk got sharp; the gentle teasing they had been engaged in with each other changed to bitchiness, a serious kind of making fun. That was Jake's clue; the girls were reacting to him. They had gotten a whiff of his manhood and were shivering for a place in his attention.

Jake left the porch rail and walked right up to a girl named Suky, the one who had been most bitter in her making fun.

"Want to show me 'round?" He didn't even smile.

Cholly held his breath, waiting for Suky to shut Jake up.

She was good at that, and well known for her sharp tongue. To his enormous surprise, she readily agreed, and even lowered her lashes. Taking courage, Cholly turned to Darlene and said, "Come on 'long. We just going down to the gully." He waited for her to screw up her face and say no, or what for, or some such thing. His feelings about her were mostly fear—fear that she would not like him, and fear that she would.

His second fear materialized. She smiled and jumped down the three leaning steps to join him. Her eyes were full of compassion, and Cholly remembered that he was the bereaved.

"If you want to," she said, "but not too far. Mama said we got to leave early, and it's getting dark."

The four of them moved away. Some of the other boys had come to the porch and were about to begin that partly hostile, partly indifferent, partly desperate mating dance. Suky, Jake, Darlene, and Cholly walked through several backyards until they came to an open field. They ran across it and came to a dry riverbed lined with green. The object of the walk was a wild vineyard where the muscadine grew. Too new, too tight to have much sugar, they were eaten anyway. None of them wanted—not then—the grape's easy relinquishing of all its dark juice. The restraint, the holding off, the promise of sweetness that had yet to unfold, excited them more than full ripeness would have done. At last their teeth were on edge, and the boys diverted themselves by pelting the girls with the grapes. Their slim black boy wrists made G clefs in the air as they executed the tosses. The chase took Cholly and Darlene away from the lip of the gully, and when they paused for breath, Jake and Suky were nowhere in sight. Darlene's white cotton dress was stained with juice.

Her big blue hair bow had come undone, and the sundown breeze was picking it up and fluttering it about her head. They were out of breath and sank down in the green-and-purple grass on the edge of the pine woods.

Cholly lay on his back panting. His mouth full of the taste of muscadine, listening to the pine needles rustling loudly in their anticipation of rain. The smell of promised rain, pine, and muscadine made him giddy. The sun had gone and pulled away its shreds of light. Turning his head to see where the moon was. Cholly caught sight of Darlene in moonlight behind him. She was huddled into a D—arms encircling drawn-up knees, on which she rested her head. Cholly could see her bloomers and the muscles of her young thighs.

"We bed' get on back," he said.

"Yeah." She stretched her legs flat on the ground and began to retie her hair ribbon. "Mama gone whup me."

"Naw she ain't."

"Uh-huh. She told me she would if I get dirty."

"You ain't dirty."

"I am too. Looka that." She dropped her hands from the ribbon and smoothed out a place on her dress where the grape stains were heaviest.

Cholly felt sorry for her; it was just as much his fault. Suddenly he realized that Aunt Jimmy was dead, for he missed the fear of being whipped. There was nobody to do it except Uncle O. V., and he was the bereaved too.

"Let me," he said. He rose to his knees facing her and tried to tie her ribbon. Darlene put her hands under his open shirt and rubbed the damp tight skin. When he looked at her in surprise, she stopped and laughed. He smiled and continued knotting the bow. She put her hands back under his shirt.

"Hold still," he said. "How I gone get this?"

She tickled his ribs with her fingertips. He giggled and grabbed his rib cage. They were on top of each other in a moment. She corkscrewing her hands into his clothes. He returning the play, digging into the neck of her dress, and then under her dress. When he got his hand in her bloomers, she suddenly stopped laughing and looked serious. Cholly, frightened, was about to take his hand away, but she held his wrist so he couldn't move it. He examined her then with his fingers, and she kissed his face and mouth. Cholly found her muscadine-lipped mouth distracting. Darlene released his head, shifted her body, and pulled down her pants. After some trouble with the buttons, Cholly dropped his pants down to his knees. Their bodies began to make sense to him, and it was not as difficult as he had thought it would be. She moaned a little, but the excitement collecting inside him made him close his eyes and regard her moans as no more than pine sighs over his head. Just as he felt an explosion threaten, Darlene froze and cried out. He thought he had hurt her, but when he looked at her face, she was staring wildly at something over his shoulder. He jerked around.

There stood two white men. One with a spirit lamp, the other with a flashlight. There was no mistake about their being white; he could smell it. Cholly jumped, trying to kneel, stand, and get his pants up all in one motion. The men had long guns.

"Hee hee hee heeeee." The snicker was a long asthmatic cough.

The other raced the flashlight all over Cholly and Darlene.

"Get on wid it, nigger," said the flashlight one.

"Sir?" said Cholly, trying to find a buttonhole.

"I said, get on wid it. An' make it good, nigger, make it good."

There was no place for Cholly's eyes to go. They slid about furtively searching for shelter, while his body remained paralyzed. The flashlight man lifted his gun down from his shoulder, and Cholly heard the clop of metal. He dropped back to his knees. Darlene had her head averted, her eyes staring out of the lamplight into the surrounding darkness and looking almost unconcerned, as though they had no part in the drama taking place around them. With a violence born of total helplessness, he pulled her dress up, lowered his trousers and underwear.

"Hee hee hee hee heeeeee."

Darlene put her hands over her face as Cholly began to simulate what had gone on before. He could do no more than make-believe. The flashlight made a moon on his behind.

"Hee hee hee hee heeee."

"Come on, coon. Faster. You ain't doing nothing for her."

"Hee hee hee hee heeee."

Cholly, moving faster, looked at Darlene. He hated her. He almost wished he could do it—hard, long, and painfully, he hated her so much. The flashlight wormed its way into his guts and turned the sweet taste of muscadine into rotten fetid bile. He stared at Darlene's hands covering her face in the moon and lamplight. They looked like baby claws.

"Hee hee hee hee heee."

Some dogs howled. "Thas them. Thas them. I know thas Old Honey."

"Yep," said the spirit lamp.

"Come on." The flashlight turned away, and one of them whistled to Honey.

"Wait," said the spirit lamp, "the coon ain't comed yet."

"Well, he have to come on his own time. Good luck, coon baby."

They crushed the pine needles underfoot. Cholly could hear them whistling for a long time, and then the dogs' answer no longer a howl, but warm excited yelps of recognition.

Cholly raised himself and in silence buttoned his trousers. Darlene did not move. Cholly wanted to strangle her, but instead he touched her leg with his foot. "We got to get, girl. Come on!"

She reached for her underwear with her eyes closed, and could not find them. The two of them patted about in the moonlight for the panties. When she found them, she put them on with the movements of an old woman. They walked away from the pine woods toward the road. He in front, she plopping along behind. It started to rain. "That's good," Cholly thought. "It will explain away our clothes."

When they got back to the house, some ten or twelve guests were still there. Jake was gone, Suky too. Some people had gone back for more helpings of food—potato pie, ribs. All were engrossed in early-night reminiscences about dreams, figures, premonitions. Their stuffed comfort was narcotic and had produced recollections and fabrications of hallucinations.

Cholly and Darlene's entrance produced only a mild stir. "Ya'll soaked, ain't you?"

Darlene's mother was only vaguely fussy. She had eaten and drunk too much. Her shoes were under her chair, and the side snaps of her dress were opened. "Girl. Come on in here. Thought I told you . . ."

Some of the guests thought they would wait for the rain to slacken. Others, who had come in wagons, thought they'd best leave now. Cholly went into the little storeroom which had been made into a bedroom for him. Three infants were sleeping on his cot. He took off his rain- and pine-soaked clothes and put on his coveralls. He didn't know where to go. Aunt Jimmy's room was out of the question, and Uncle O. V. and his wife would be using it later anyway. He took a quilt from a trunk, spread it on the floor, and lay down. Somebody was brewing coffee, and he had a sharp craving for it, just before falling asleep.

The next day was cleaning-out day, settling accounts, distributing Aunt Jimmy's goods. Mouths were set in downward crescents, eyes veiled, feet tentative.

Cholly floated about aimlessly, doing chores as he was told. All the glamour and warmth the adults had given him on the previous day were replaced by a sharpness that agreed with his mood. He could think only of the flashlight, the muscadines, and Darlene's hands. And when he was not thinking of them, the vacancy in his head was like the space left by a newly pulled tooth still conscious of the rottenness that had once filled it. Afraid of running into Darlene, he would not go far from the house, but neither could he endure the atmosphere of his dead Aunt's house. The picking through her things, the comments on the "condition" of her goods. Sullen, irritable, he cultivated his hatred of Darlene. Never did he once consider directing his hatred toward the hunters. Such an emotion would have destroyed him. They were big, white, armed men. He was small, black, helpless. His subconscious knew what his conscious mind did not guess—that hating them would have consumed him, burned him up like a piece of soft coal, leaving only flakes of ash and a question mark of smoke. He was, in time, to discover that hatred of white men—but not now. Not in impotence but later, when the hatred could find sweet expression. For now, he hated the one who had created the situation, the one who bore witness to his failure, his impotence. The one whom he had not been able to protect, to spare, to cover from the round moon glow of the flashlight. The hee-hee-hee's. He recalled Darlene's dripping hair ribbon, flapping against her face as they walked back in silence in the rain. The loathing that galloped through him made him tremble. There was no one to talk to. Old Blue was too drunk too often these days to make sense. Besides, Cholly doubted if he could reveal his shame to Blue. He would have to lie a little to tell Blue, Blue the woman-killer. It seemed to him that lonely was much better than alone.

The day Cholly's uncle was ready to leave, when everything was packed, when the quarrels about who gets what had seethed down to a sticking gravy on everybody's tongue, Cholly sat on the back porch waiting. It had occurred to him that Darlene might be pregnant. It was a wildly irrational, completely uninformed idea, but the fear it produced was complete enough.

He had to get away. Never mind the fact that he was leaving that very day. A town or two away was not far enough, especially since he did not like or trust his uncle, and Darlene's mother could surely find him, and Uncle O. V. would turn him over to her. Cholly knew it was wrong to run out on a pregnant girl, and recalled, with sympathy, that his father had done just that. Now he understood. He knew then what he must do—find his father. His father would understand. Aunt Jimmy said he had gone to Macon.

With no more thought than a chick leaving its shell, he stepped off the porch. He had gotten a little way when he remembered the treasure; Aunt Jimmy had left something, and he had forgotten all about it. In a stove flue no longer used, she had hidden a little meal bag which she called her treasure. He slipped into the house and found the room empty. Digging into the flue, he encountered webs and soot, and then the soft bag. He sorted the money; fourteen one-dollar bills, two two-dollar bills, and lots of silver change . . . twenty-three dollars in all. Surely that would be enough to get to Macon. What a good, strong-sounding word, *Macon*.

Running away from home for a Georgia black boy was not a great problem. You just sneaked away and started walking. When night came you slept in a barn, if there were no dogs, a cane field, or an empty sawmill. You ate from the ground and bought root beer and licorice in little country stores. There was always an easy tale of woe to tell inquiring black adults, and whites didn't care, unless they were looking for sport.

When he was several days away, he could go to the back door of nice houses and tell the black cook or white mistress that he wanted a job weeding, plowing, picking, cleaning, and that he lived nearby. A week or more there, and he could take off. He lived this way through the turn of summer, and only the following October did he reach a town big enough to have a regular bus station. Dry-mouthed with excitement and apprehension, he went to the colored side of the counter to buy his ticket.

"How much to Macon, sir?"

"Eleven dollars. Five-fifty for children under twelve."

Cholly had twelve dollars and four cents.

"How old you be?"

"Just on twelve, sir, but my mama only give me ten dollars."

"You jest about the biggest twelve I ever seed."

"Please, sir, I got to get to Macon. My mama's sick."

"Thought you said you mama give you ten dollars."

"That's my play mama. My real mama is in Macon, sir."

"I reckon I knows a lying nigger when I sees one, but jest in case you ain't, jest in case one of them mammies is really dyin' and wants to see her little old smoke before she meets her maker, I gone do it."

Cholly heard nothing. The insults were part of the nuisances of life, like lice. He was happier than he had ever remembered being, except that time with Blue and the watermelon. The bus wasn't leaving for four hours, and the minutes of those hours struggled like gnats on fly paper—dying slow, exhausted with the fight to stay alive. Cholly was afraid to stir, even to relieve himself. The bus might leave while he was gone. Finally, rigid with constipation, he boarded the bus to Macon.

He found a window seat in the back all to himself, and all of Georgia slid before his eyes, until the sun shrugged out of sight. Even in the dark, he hungered to see, and only after the fiercest fight to keep his eyes open did he fall asleep. When he awoke it was very well into day, and a fat black lady was nudging him with a biscuit gashed with cold bacon. With the taste of bacon still in his teeth, they sidled into Macon.

. . .

At the end of the alley he could see men clustered like grapes. One large whooping voice spiraled over the heads of the bended forms. The kneeling forms, the leaning forms, all intent on one ground spot. As he came closer, he inhaled a rife and stimulating man smell. The men were gathered, just as the man in the pool hall had said, for and about dice and money. Each figure was decorated some way with the slight pieces of green. Some of them had separated their money, folded the bills around their fingers, clenched the fingers into fists, so the neat ends of the money stuck out in a blend of daintiness and violence. Others had stacked their bills, creased them down the middle, and held the wad as though they were about to deal cards. Still others had left their money in loosely crumpled balls. One man had money sticking out from under his cap. Another stroked his bills with a thumb and forefinger. There was more money in those black hands than Cholly had ever seen before. He shared their excitement, and the dry-mouthed apprehension on meeting his father gave way to the saliva flow of excitement. He glanced at the faces, looking for the one who might be his father. How would he know him? Would he look like a larger version of himself? At that moment Cholly could not remember what his own self looked like. He only knew he was fourteen years old, black, and already six feet tall. He searched the faces and saw only eyes, pleading eyes, cold eyes, eyes gone flat with malice, others laced with fear—all focused on the movement of a pair of dice that one man was throwing, snatching up, and throwing again. Chanting a kind of litany to which the others responded, rubbing the dice as though they were two hot coals, he whispered to them. Then with a whoop the cubes flew from his hand to a chorus of amazements and disappointments. Then the thrower scooped up money, and someone shouted, "Take it and crawl, you water dog, you, the best I know." There was some laughter, and a noticeable release of tension, during which some men exchanged money.

Cholly tapped an old white-haired man on the back.

"Can you tell me is Samson Fuller 'round here somewhere?"

"Fuller?" The name was familiar to the man's tongue. "I don't know, he here somewhere. They he is. In the brown jacket." The man pointed.

A man in a light-brown jacket stood at the far end of the group. He was gesturing in a quarrelsome, agitated manner with another man. Both of them had folded their faces in anger. Cholly edged around to where they stood, hardly believing he was at the end of his journey. There was his father, a man like any other man, but there indeed were his eyes, his mouth, his whole head. His shoulders lurked beneath that jacket, his voice, his hands—all real. They existed, really existed, somewhere. Right here. Cholly had always thought of his father as a giant of a man, so when he was very close it was with a shock that he discovered that he was taller than his father. In fact, he was staring at a balding spot on his father's head, which he suddenly wanted to stroke. While thus fascinated by the pitiable clean space hedged around by neglected tufts of wool, the man turned a hard, belligerent face to him.

"What you want, boy?"

"Uh. I mean . . . is you Samson Fuller?"

"Who sent you?"

"Huh?"

"You Melba's boy?"

"No, sir, I'm . . ." Cholly blinked. He could not remember his mother's name. Had he ever known it? What could he say? Whose boy was he? He couldn't say, "I'm your boy." That sounded disrespectful.

The man was impatient. "Something wrong with your head? Who told you to come after me?"

"Nobody." Cholly's hands were sweating. The man's eyes frightened him. "I just thought . . . I mean, I was just wandering around, and, uh, my name is Cholly. . . ."

But Fuller had turned back to the game that was about to begin anew. He bent down to toss a bill on the ground, and waited for a throw. When it was gone, he stood up and in a vexed and whiny voice shouted at Cholly, "Tell that bitch she get her money. Now, get the fuck outta my face!"

Cholly was a long time picking his foot up from the ground. He was trying to back up and walk away. Only with extreme effort could he get the first muscle to cooperate. When it did, he walked back up the alley, out of its shade, toward the blazing light of the street. As he emerged into the sun, he felt something in his legs give way. An orange crate with a picture of clasping hands pasted on its side was upended on the sidewalk. Cholly sat down on it. The sunshine dropped like honey on his head. A horse-drawn fruit wagon went by, its driver singing: "Fresh from the vine, sweet as sugar, red as wine."

Noises seemed to increase in volume. The clic-cloc of the women's heels, the laughter of idling men in doorways. There was a streetcar somewhere. Cholly sat. He knew if he was very still he would be all right. But then the trace of pain edged his eyes, and he had to use everything to send it away. If he was very still, he thought, and kept his eyes on one thing, the tears would not come. So he sat in the dripping honey sun, pulling every nerve and muscle into service to stop the fall of water from his eyes. While straining in this way, focusing every erg of energy on his eyes, his bowels suddenly opened up, and before he could realize what he knew, liquid stools were running down his legs. At the mouth of the alley where his father was, on an orange crate in the sun, on a street full of grown men and women, he had soiled himself like a baby.

In panic he wondered should he wait there, not moving until nighttime? No. His father would surely emerge and see him and laugh. Oh, Lord. He would laugh. Everybody would laugh. There was only one thing to do.

Cholly ran down the street, aware only of silence. People's mouths moved, their feet moved, a car jugged by—but with no sound. A door slammed in perfect soundlessness. His own feet made no sound. The air seemed to strangle him, hold him back. He was pushing through a world of invisible pine sap that threatened to smother him. Still he ran, seeing only silent moving things, until he came to the end of buildings, the beginning of open space, and saw the Ocmulgee River winding ahead. He scooted down a gravelly slope to a pier jutting out over the shallow water. Finding the deepest shadow under the pier, he crouched in it, behind one of the posts. He remained knotted there in fetal position, paralyzed, his fists covering his eyes, for a long time. No sound, no sight, only darkness and heat and the press of his knuckles on his eyelids. He even forgot his messed-up trousers.

Evening came. The dark, the warmth, the quiet, enclosed Cholly like the skin and flesh of an elderberry protecting its own seed.

Cholly stirred. The ache in his head was all he felt. Soon, like bright bits of glass, the events of that afternoon cut into him. At first he saw only money in black fingers, then he thought he was sitting on an uncomfortable chair, but when he looked, it turned out to be the head of a man, a head with a bald spot the size of an orange. When finally these bits merged into full memory, Cholly began to smell himself. He stood up and found himself weak, trembling, and dizzy. He leaned for a moment on the pier post, then took off his pants, underwear, socks, and shoes. He rubbed handfuls of dirt on his shoes; then he crawled to the river edge. He had to find the water's beginning with his hands, for he could not see it clearly. Slowly he swirled his clothes in the water and rubbed them until he thought they were clean. Back near his post, he took off his shirt and wrapped it around his waist, then spread his trousers and underwear on the ground. He squatted down and picked at the rotted wood of the pier. Suddenly he thought of his Aunt Jimmy, her asafetida bag, her four gold teeth, and the purple rag she wore around her head. With a longing that almost split him open, he thought of her handing him a bit of smoked hock out of her dish. He remembered just how she held it—clumsy-like, in three fingers, but with so much affection. No words, just picking up a bit of meat and holding it out to him. And then the tears rushed down his cheeks, to make a bouquet under his chin.

Three women are leaning out of two windows. They see the long clean neck of a new young boy and call to him. He goes to where they are. Inside, it is dark and warm. They give him lemonade in a Mason jar. As he drinks, their eyes float up to him through the bottom of the jar, through the slick sweet water. They give him back his manhood, which he takes aimlessly.

The pieces of Cholly's life could become coherent only in the head of a musician. Only those who talk their talk through the gold of curved metal, or in the touch of black-and-white rectangles and taut skins and strings echoing from wooden corridors, could give true form to his life. Only they would know how to connect the heart of a red watermelon to the asafetida bag to the muscadine to the flashlight on his behind to the fists of money to the lemonade in a Mason jar to a man called Blue and come up with what all of that meant in joy, in pain, in anger, in love, and give it its final and pervading ache of freedom. Only a musician would sense, know, without even knowing that he knew, that Cholly was free. Dangerously free. Free to feel whatever he felt—fear, guilt, shame, love, grief, pity. Free to be tender or violent, to whistle or weep. Free to sleep in doorways or between the white sheets of a singing woman. Free to take a job, free to leave it. He could go to jail and not feel imprisoned, for he had already seen the furtiveness in the eyes of his jailer, free to say, "No, suh," and smile, for he had already killed three white men. Free to take a woman's insults, for his body had already conquered hers. Free even to knock her in the head, for he had already cradled that head in his arms. Free to be gentle when she was sick, or mop her floor, for she knew what and where his maleness was. He was free to drink himself into a silly helplessness, for he had already been a gandy dancer, done thirty days on a chain gang, and picked a woman's bullet out of the calf of his leg. He was free to live his fantasies, and free even to die, the how and the when of which held no interest for him. In those days, Cholly was truly free. Abandoned in a junk heap by his mother, rejected for a crap game by his father, there was nothing more to lose. He was alone with his own perceptions and appetites, and they alone interested him.

It was in this godlike state that he met Pauline Williams. And it was Pauline, or rather marrying her, that did for him what the flashlight did not do. The constantness, varietylessness, the sheer weight of sameness drove him to despair and froze his imagination. To be required to sleep with the same woman forever was a curious and unnatural idea to him; to be expected to dredge up enthusiasms for old acts, and routine ploys; he wondered at the arrogance of the female. When he had met Pauline in Kentucky, she was hanging over a fence scratching herself with a broken foot. The neatness, the charm, the joy he awakened in her made him want to nest with her. He had yet to discover what destroyed that desire. But he did not dwell on it. He thought rather of whatever had happened to the curiosity he used to feel. Nothing, nothing, interested him now. Not himself, not other people. Only in drink was there some break, some floodlight, and when that closed, there was oblivion.

But the aspect of married life that dumbfounded him and rendered him totally disfunctional was the appearance of children. Having no idea of how to raise children, and having never watched any parent raise himself, he could not even comprehend what such a relationship should be. Had he been interested in the accumulation of things, he could have thought of them as his material heirs; had he needed to prove himself to some nameless "others," he could have wanted them to excel in his own image and for his own sake. Had he not been alone in the world since he was thirteen, knowing only a dying old woman who felt responsible for him, but whose age, sex, and interests were so remote from his own, he might have felt a stable connection between himself and the children. As it was, he reacted to them, and his reactions were based on what he felt at the moment.

So it was on a Saturday afternoon, in the thin light of spring, he staggered home reeling drunk and saw his daughter in the kitchen.

She was washing dishes. Her small back hunched over the sink. Cholly saw her dimly and could not tell what he saw or what he felt. Then he became aware that he was uncomfortable; next he felt the discomfort dissolve into pleasure. The sequence of his emotions was revulsion, guilt, pity, then love. His revulsion was a reaction to her young, helpless, hopeless presence. Her back hunched that way; her head to one side as though crouching from a permanent and unrelieved blow. Why did she have to look so whipped? She was a child—unburdened—why wasn't she happy? The clear statement of her misery was an accusation. He wanted to break her neck—but tenderly. Guilt and impotence rose in a bilious duet. What could he do for her—ever? What give her? What say to her? What could a burned-out black man say to the hunched back of his eleven-year-old daughter? If he looked into her face, he would see those haunted, loving eyes. The hauntedness would irritate him—the love would move him to fury. How dare she love him? Hadn't she any sense at all? What was he supposed to do about that? Return it? How? What could his calloused hands produce to make her smile? What of his knowledge of the world and of life could be useful to her? What could his heavy arms and befuddled brain accomplish that would earn him his own respect, that would in turn allow him to accept her love? His hatred of her slimed in his stomach and threatened to become vomit. But just before the puke moved from anticipation to sensation, she shifted her weight and stood on one foot scratching the back of her calf with her toe. It was a quiet and pitiful gesture. Her hands were going around and around a frying pan, scraping flecks of black into cold, greasy dishwater. The timid, tucked-in look of the scratching toe—that was what Pauline was doing the first time he saw her in Kentucky. Leaning over a fence staring at nothing in particular. The creamy toe of her bare foot scratching a velvet leg. It was such a small and simple gesture, but it filled him then with a wondering softness. Not the usual lust to part tight legs with his own, but a tenderness, a protectiveness. A desire to cover her foot with his hand and gently nibble away the itch from the calf with his teeth. He did it then, and started Pauline into laughter. He did it now.

The tenderness welled up in him, and he sank to his knees, his eyes on the foot of his daughter. Crawling on all fours toward her, he raised his hand and caught the foot in an upward stroke. Pecola lost her balance and was about to career to the floor. Cholly raised his other hand to her hips to save her from falling. He put his head down and nibbled at the back of her leg. His mouth trembled at the firm sweetness of the flesh. He closed his eyes, letting his fingers dig into her waist. The rigidness of her shocked body, the silence of her stunned throat, was better than Pauline's easy laughter had been. The confused mixture of his memories of Pauline and the doing of a wild and forbidden thing excited him, and a bolt of desire ran down his genitals, giving it length, and softening the lips of his anus. Surrounding all of this lust was a border of politeness. He wanted to fuck her—tenderly. But the tenderness would not hold. The tightness of her vagina was more than he could bear. His soul seemed to slip down to his guts and fly out into her, and the gigantic thrust he made into her then provoked the only sound she made—a hollow suck of air in the back of her throat. Like the rapid loss of air from a circus balloon.

Following the disintegration—the falling away—of sexual desire, he was conscious of her wet, soapy hands on his wrists, the fingers clenching, but whether her grip was from a hopeless but stubborn struggle to be free, or from some other emotion, he could not tell.

Removing himself from her was so painful to him he cut it short and snatched his genitals out of the dry harbor of her vagina. She appeared to have fainted. Cholly stood up and could see only her grayish panties, so sad and limp around her ankles. Again the hatred mixed with tenderness. The hatred would not let him pick her up, the tenderness forced him to cover her.

So when the child regained consciousness, she was lying on the kitchen floor under a heavy quilt, trying to connect the pain between her legs with the face of her mother looming over her.

SEETHEDOGBOWWOWGOESTHEDOG
DOYOUWANTTOPLAYDOYOUWANT
TOPLAYWITHJANESEETHEDOGRUNR

Once there was an old man who loved things, for the slightest contact with people produced in him a faint but persistent nausea. He could not remember when this distaste began, nor could he remember ever being free of it. As a young boy he had been greatly disturbed by this revulsion which others did not seem to share, but having got a fine education, he learned, among other things, the word "misanthrope." Knowing his label provided him with both comfort and courage, he believed that to name an evil was to neutralize if not annihilate it. Then, too, he had read several books and made the acquaintance of several great misanthropes of the ages, whose spiritual company soothed him and provided him with yardsticks for measuring his whims, his yearnings, and his antipathies. Moreover, he found misanthropy an excellent means of developing character: when he subdued his revulsion and occasionally touched, helped, counseled, or befriended somebody, he was able to think of his behavior as generous and his intentions as noble. When he was enraged by some human effort or flaw, he was able to regard himself as discriminating, fastidious, and full of nice scruples.

As in the case of many misanthropes, his disdain for people led him into a profession designed to serve them. He was engaged in a line of work that was dependent solely on his ability to win the trust of others, and one in which the most intimate relationships were necessary. Having dallied with the priesthood in the Anglican Church, he abandoned it to become a caseworker. Time and misfortune, however, conspired against him, and he settled finally on a profession that brought him both freedom and satisfaction. He became a "Reader, Adviser, and Interpreter of Dreams." It was a profession that suited him well. His hours were his own, the competition was slight, the clientele was already persuaded and therefore manageable, and he had numerous opportunities to witness human stupidity without sharing it or being compromised by it, and to nurture his fastidiousness by viewing physical decay. Although his income was small, he had no taste for luxury—his experience in the monastery had solidified his natural asceticism while it developed his preference for solitude. Celibacy was a haven, silence a shield.

All his life he had a fondness for things—not the acquisition of wealth or beautiful objects, but a genuine love of worn objects: a coffee pot that had been his mother's, a welcome mat from the door of a rooming house he once lived in, a quilt from a Salvation Army store counter. It was as though his disdain of human contact had converted itself into a craving for things humans had touched. The residue of the human spirit smeared on inanimate objects was all he could withstand of humanity. To contemplate, for example, evidence of human footsteps on the mat—absorb the smell of the quilt and wallow in the sweet certainty that many bodies had sweated, slept, dreamed, made love, been ill, and even died under it. Wherever he went, he took along his things, and was always searching for others. This thirst for worn things led to casual but habitual examinations of trash barrels in alleys and wastebaskets in public places. . . .

All in all, his personality was an arabesque: intricate, symmetrical, balanced, and tightly constructed—except for one flaw. The careful design was marred occasionally by rare but keen sexual cravings.

He could have been an active homosexual but lacked the courage. Bestiality did not occur to him, and sodomy was quite out of the question, for he did not experience sustained erections and could not endure the thought of somebody else's. And besides, the one thing that disgusted him more than entering and caressing a woman was caressing and being caressed by a man. In any case, his cravings, although intense, never relished physical contact. He abhorred flesh on flesh. Body odor, breath odor, overwhelmed him. The sight of dried matter in the corner of the eye, decayed or missing teeth, ear wax, blackheads, moles, blisters, skin crusts—all the natural excretions and protections the body was capable of—disquieted him. His attentions therefore gradually settled on those humans whose bodies were least offensive—children. And since he was too diffident to confront homosexuality, and since little boys were insulting, scary, and stubborn, he further limited his interests to little girls. They were usually manageable and frequently seductive. His sexuality was anything but lewd; his patronage of little girls smacked of innocence and was associated in his mind with cleanliness. He was what one might call a very clean old man.

A cinnamon-eyed West Indian with lightly browned skin.

Although his given name was printed on the sign in his kitchen window, and on the business cards he circulated, he was called by the townspeople Soaphead Church. No one knew where the "Church" part came from—perhaps somebody's recollection of his days as a guest preacher—those reverends who had been called but who had no flock or coop, and were constantly visiting other churches, sitting on the altar with the host preacher. But everybody knew what "Soaphead" meant—the tight, curly hair that took on and held a sheen and wave when pomaded with soap lather. A sort of primitive process.

He had been reared in a family proud of its academic accomplishments and its mixed blood—in fact, they believed the former was based on the latter. A Sir Whitcomb, some decaying British nobleman, who chose to disintegrate under a sun more easeful than England's, had introduced the white strain into the family in the early 1800's. Being a gentleman by order of the King, he had done the civilized thing for his mulatto bastard—provided it with three hundred pounds sterling, to the great satisfaction of the bastard's mother, who felt that fortune had smiled on her. The bastard too was grateful, and regarded as his life's goal the hoarding of this white strain. He bestowed his favors on a fifteen-year-old girl of similar parentage. She, like a good Victorian parody, learned from her husband all that was worth learning—to separate herself in body, mind, and spirit from all that suggested Africa; to cultivate the habits, tastes, preferences that her absent father-in-law and foolish mother-in-law would have approved.

They transferred this Anglophilia to their six children and sixteen grandchildren. Except for an occasional and unaccountable insurgent who chose a restive black, they married "up," lightening the family complexion and thinning out the family features.

With the confidence born of a conviction of superiority, they performed well at schools. They were industrious, orderly, and energetic, hoping to prove beyond a doubt De Gobineau's hypothesis that "all civilizations derive from the white race, that none can exist without its help, and that a society is great and brilliant only so far as it preserves the blood of the noble group that created it." Thus, they were seldom overlooked by schoolmasters who recommended promising students for study abroad. The men studied medicine, law, theology, and emerged repeatedly in the powerless government offices available to the native population. That they were corrupt in public and private practice, both lecherous and lascivious, was considered their noble right, and thoroughly enjoyed by most of the less gifted population.

As the years passed, due to the carelessness of some of the Whitcomb brothers, it became difficult to maintain their whiteness, and some distant and some not so distant relatives married each other. No obviously bad effects were noticed from these ill-advised unions, but one or two old maids or gardener boys marked a weakening of faculties and a disposition toward eccentricity in some of the children. Some flaw outside the usual alcoholism and lechery. They blamed the flaw on intermarriage with the family, however, not on the original genes of the decaying lord. In any case, there were flukes. No more than in any other family, to be sure, but more dangerous because more powerful. One of them was a religious fanatic who founded his own secret sect and fathered four sons, one of whom became a schoolmaster known for the precision of his justice and the control in his violence. This schoolmaster married a sweet, indolent half-Chinese girl for whom the fatigue of bearing a son was too much. She died soon after childbirth. Her son, named Elihue Micah Whitcomb, provided the schoolmaster with ample opportunity to work out his theories of education, discipline, and the good life. Little Elihue learned everything he needed to know well, particularly the fine art of self-deception. He read greedily but understood selectively, choosing the bits and pieces of other men's ideas that supported whatever predilection he had at the moment. Thus he chose to remember Hamlet's abuse of Ophelia, but not Christ's love of Mary Magdalene; Hamlet's frivolous politics, but not Christ's serious anarchy. He noticed Gibbon's acidity, but not his tolerance, Othello's love for the fair Desdemona, but not Iago's perverted love of Othello. The works he admired most were Dante's; those he despised most were Dostoyevsky's. For all his exposure to the best minds of the Western world, he allowed only the narrowest interpretation to touch him. He responded to his father's controlled violence by developing hard habits and a soft imagination. A hatred of, and fascination with, any hint of disorder or decay.

At seventeen, however, he met his Beatrice, who was three years his senior. A lovely, laughing big-legged girl who worked as a clerk in a Chinese department store. Velma. So strong was her affection and zest for life, she did not eliminate the frail, sickly Elihue from it. She found his fastidiousness and complete lack of humor touching and longed to introduce him to the idea of delight. He resisted the introduction, but she married him anyway, only to discover that he was suffering from and enjoying an invincible melancholy. When she learned two months into the marriage how important his melancholy was to him, that he was very interested in altering her joy to a more academic gloom, that he equated lovemaking with communion and the Holy Grail, she simply left. She had not lived by the sea all those years, listened to the wharfman's songs all that time, to spend her life in the soundless cave of Elihue's mind.

He never got over her desertion. She was to have been the answer to his unstated, unacknowledged question—where was the life to counter the encroaching nonlife? Velma was to rescue him from the nonlife he had learned on the flat side of his father's belt. But he resisted her with such skill that she was finally driven out to escape the inevitable boredom produced by such a dainty life.

Young Elihue was saved from visible shattering by the steady hand of his father, who reminded him of the family's reputation and Velma's questionable one. He then pursued his studies with more vigor than before and decided at last to enter the ministry. When he was advised that he had no avocation, he left the island, came to America to study the then budding field of psychiatry. But the subject required too much truth, too many confrontations, and offered too little support to a failing ego. He drifted into sociology, then physical therapy. This diverse education continued for six years, when his father refused to support him any longer, until he "found" himself. Elihue, not knowing where to look, was thrown back on his own devices, and "found" himself quite unable to earn money. He began to sink into a rapidly fraying gentility, punctuated with a few of the white-collar occupations available to black people, regardless of their noble bloodlines, in America: desk clerk at a colored hotel in Chicago, insurance agent, traveling salesman for a cosmetics firm catering to blacks. He finally settled in Lorain, Ohio, in 1931, palming himself off as a minister, and inspiring awe with the way he spoke English. The women of the town early discovered his celibacy, and not being able to comprehend his rejection of them, decided that he was supernatural rather than unnatural.

Once he understood their decision, he quickly followed through, accepting the name (Soaphead Church) and the role they had given him. He rented a kind of back-room apartment from a deeply religious old lady named Bertha Reese. She was clean, quiet, and very close to total deafness. The lodgings were ideal in every way but one. Bertha Reese had an old dog, Bob, who, although as deaf and quiet as she, was not as clean. He slept most of his days away on the back porch, which was Elihue's entrance. The dog was too old to be of any use, and Bertha Reese had not the strength or presence of mind to care for him properly. She fed him, and watered him, left him alone. The dog was mangy; his exhausted eyes ran with a sea-green matter around which gnats and flies clustered. Soaphead was revolted by Bob and wished he would hurry up and die. He regarded this wish for the dog's death as humane, for he could not bear, he told himself, to see anything suffer. It did not occur to him that he was really concerned about his own suffering, since the dog had adjusted himself to frailty and old age. Soaphead finally determined to put an end to the animal's misery, and bought some poison with which to do it. Only the horror of having to go near him had prevented Soaphead from completing his mission. He waited for rage or blinding revulsion to spur him.

Living there among his worn things, rising early every morning from dreamless sleeps, he counseled those who sought his advice.

His business was dread. People came to him in dread, whispered in dread, wept and pleaded in dread. And dread was what he counseled.

Singly they found their way to his door, wrapped each in a shroud stitched with anger, yearning, pride, vengeance, loneliness, misery, defeat, and hunger. They asked for the simplest of things: love, health, and money. Make him love me. Tell me what this dream means. Help me get rid of this woman. Make my mother give me back my clothes. Stop my left hand from shaking. Keep my baby's ghost off the stove. Break so-and-so's fix. To all of these requests he addressed himself. His practice was to do what he was bid—not to suggest to a party that perhaps the request was unfair, mean, or hopeless.

With only occasional, and increasingly rare, encounters with the little girls he could persuade to be entertained by him, he lived rather peaceably among his things, admitting to no regrets. He was aware, of course, that something was awry in his life, and all lives, but put the problem where it belonged, at the foot of the Originator of Life. He believed that since decay, vice, filth, and disorder were pervasive, they must be in the Nature of Things. Evil existed because God had created it. He, God, had made a sloven and unforgivable error in judgment: designing an imperfect universe. Theologians justified the presence of corruption as a means by which men strove, were tested, and triumphed. A triumph of cosmic neatness. But this neatness, the neatness of Dante, was in the orderly sectioning and segregating of all levels of evil and decay. In the world it was not so. The most exquisite-looking ladies sat on toilets, and the most dreadful-looking had pure and holy yearnings. God had done a poor job, and Soaphead suspected that he himself could have done better. It was in fact a pity that the Maker had not sought his counsel.

Soaphead was reflecting once again on these thoughts one late hot afternoon when he heard a tap on his door. Opening it, he saw a little girl, quite unknown to him. She was about twelve or so, he thought, and seemed to him pitifully unattractive. When he asked her what she wanted, she did not answer, but held out to him one of his cards advertising his gifts and services: "If you are overcome with trouble and conditions that are not natural, I can remove them; Overcome Spells, Bad Luck, and Evil Influences. Remember, I am a true Spiritualist and Psychic Reader, born with power, and I will help you. Satisfaction in one visit. During many years of practice I have brought together many in marriage and reunited many who were separated. If you are unhappy, discouraged, or in distress, I can help you. Does bad luck seem to follow you? Has the one you love changed? I can tell you why. I will tell you who your enemies and friends are, and if the one you love is true or false. If you are sick, I can show you the way to health. I locate lost and stolen articles. Satisfaction guaranteed."

Soaphead Church told her to come in.

"What can I do for you, my child?"

She stood there, her hands folded across her stomach, a little protruding pot of tummy. "Maybe. Maybe you can do it for me."

"Do what for you?"

"I can't go to school no more. And I thought maybe you could help me."

"Help you how? Tell me. Don't be frightened."

"My eyes."

"What about your eyes?"

"I want them blue."

Soaphead pursed his lips, and let his tongue stroke a gold inlay. He thought it was at once the most fantastic and the most logical petition he had ever received. Here was an ugly little girl asking for beauty. A surge of love and understanding swept through him, but was quickly replaced by anger. Anger that he was powerless to help her. Of all the wishes people had brought him—money, love, revenge—this seemed to him the most poignant and the one most deserving of fulfillment. A little black girl who wanted to rise up out of the pit of her blackness and see the world with blue eyes. His outrage grew and felt like power. For the first time he honestly wished he could work miracles. Never before had he really wanted the true and holy power—only the power to make others believe he had it. It seemed so sad, so frivolous, that mere mortality, not judgment, kept him from it. Or did it?

With a trembling hand he made the sign of the cross over her. His flesh crawled; in that hot, dim little room of worn things, he was chilled.

"I can do nothing for you, my child. I am not a magician. I work only through the Lord. He sometimes uses me to help people. All I can do is offer myself to Him as the instrument through which he works. If He wants your wish granted, He will do it."

Soaphead walked to the window, his back to the girl. His mind raced, stumbled, and raced again. How to frame the next sentence? How to hang on to the feeling of power. His eye fell on old Bob sleeping on the porch.

"We must make, ah, some offering, that is, some contact with nature. Perhaps some simple creature might be the vehicle through which He will speak. Let us see."

He knelt down at the window, and moved his lips. After what seemed a suitable length of time, he rose and went to the icebox that stood near the other window. From it he removed a small packet wrapped in pinkish butcher paper. From a shelf he took a small brown bottle and sprinkled some of its contents on the substance inside the paper. He put the packet, partly opened, on the table.

"Take this food and give it to the creature sleeping on the porch. Make sure he eats it. And mark well how he behaves. If nothing happens, you will know that God has refused you. If the animal behaves strangely, your wish will be granted on the day following this one."

The girl picked up the packet; the odor of the dark, sticky meat made her want to vomit. She put a hand on her stomach.

"Courage. Courage, my child. These things are not granted to faint hearts."

She nodded and swallowed visibly, holding down the vomit. Soaphead opened the door, and she stepped over the threshold.

"Good-bye, God bless," he said and quickly shut the door. At the window he stood watching her, his eyebrows pulled together into waves of compassion, his tongue fondling the worn gold in his upper jaw. He saw the girl bending down to the sleeping dog, who, at her touch, opened one liquid eye, matted in the corners with what looked like green glue. She reached out and touched the dog's head, stroking him gently. She placed the meat on the floor of the porch, near his nose. The odor roused him; he lifted his head, and got up to smell it better. He ate it in three or four gulps. The girl stroked his head again, and the dog looked up at her with soft triangle eyes. Suddenly he coughed, the cough of a phlegmy old man—and got to his feet. The girl jumped. The dog gagged, his mouth chomping the air, and promptly fell down. He tried to raise himself, could not, tried again and half-fell down the steps. Choking, stumbling, he moved like a broken toy around the yard. The girl's mouth was open, a little petal of tongue showing. She made a wild, pointless gesture with one hand and then covered her mouth with both hands. She was trying not to vomit. The dog fell again, a spasm jerking his body. Then he was quiet. The girl's hands covering her mouth, she backed away a few feet, then turned, ran out of the yard and down the walk.

Soaphead Church went to the table. He sat down, with folded hands balancing his forehead on the balls of his thumbs. Then he rose and went to a tiny night table with a drawer, from which he took paper and a fountain pen. A bottle of ink was on the same shelf that held the poison. With these things he sat again at the table. Slowly, carefully, relishing his penmanship, he wrote the following letter:

Att: TO HE WHO GREATLY ENNOBLED HUMAN NATURE BY CREATING IT
Dear God:
The Purpose of this letter is to familiarize you with facts which either have escaped your notice, or which you have chosen to ignore.

Once upon a time I lived greenly and youngish on one of your islands. An island of the archipelago in the

South Atlantic between North and South America, enclosing the Caribbean Sea and the Gulf of Mexico: divided into the Greater Antilles, the Lesser Antilles, and the Bahama Islands. Not the Windward or Leeward Island colonies, mark you, but within, of course, the Greater of the two Antilles (while the precision of my prose may be, at times, laborious, it is necessary that I identify myself to you clearly).

Now.

We in this colony took as our own the most dramatic, and the most obvious, of our white masters' characteristics, which were, of course, their worst. In retaining the identity of our race, we held fast to those characteristics most gratifying to sustain and least troublesome to maintain. Consequently we were not royal but snobbish, not aristocratic but class-conscious; we believed authority was cruelty to our inferiors, and education was being at school. We mistook violence for passion, indolence for leisure, and thought recklessness was freedom. We raised our children and reared our crops; we let infants grow, and property develop. Our manhood was defined by acquisitions. Our womanhood by acquiescence. And the smell of your fruit and the labor of your days we abhorred.

This morning, before the little black girl came, I cried—for Velma. Oh, not aloud. There is no wind to carry, bear, or even refuse to bear, a sound so heavy with regret. But in my silent own lone way, I cried—for Velma. You need to know about Velma to understand what I did today.

She (Velma) left me the way people leave a hotel room. A hotel room is a place to be when you are doing something else. Of itself it is of no consequence to one's major scheme. A hotel room is convenient. But its convenience is limited to the time you need it while you are in that particular town on that particular business; you hope it is comfortable, but prefer, rather, that it be anonymous. It is not, after all, where you *live*.

When you no longer need it, you pay a little something for its use; say, "Thank you, sir," and when your business in that town is over, you go away from that room. Does anybody regret leaving a hotel room? Does anybody, who has a home, a real home somewhere, want to stay there? Does anybody look back with affection, or even disgust, at a hotel room when they leave it? You can only love or despise whatever *living* was done in that room. But the room itself? But you take a souvenir. Not, oh, not, to remember the room. To remember, rather, the time and the place of your business, your adventure. What can anyone feel for a hotel room? One doesn't any more feel for a hotel room than one expects a hotel room to feel for its occupant.

That, heavenly, heavenly Father, was how she left me; or rather, she never left me, because she was never ever there.

You remember, do you, how and of what we are made? Let me tell you now about the breasts of little girls. I apologize for the inappropriateness (is that it?), the imbalance of loving them at awkward times of day, and in awkward places, and the tastelessness of loving those which belonged to members of my family. Do I have to apologize for loving strangers?

But you too are amiss here, Lord. How, why, did you allow it to happen? How is it I could lift my eyes from

the contemplation of Your Body and fall deeply into
the contemplation of theirs? The buds. The buds on
some of these saplings. They were mean, you know,
mean and tender. Mean little buds resisting the touch,
springing like rubber. But aggressive. Daring me to
touch. Commanding me to touch. Not a bit shy, as
you'd suppose. They stuck out at me, oh yes, at me.
Slender-chested, finger-chested lassies. Have you ever
seen them, Lord? I mean, really seen them? One could
not see them and not love them. You who made them
must have considered them lovely even as an idea—
how much more lovely is the manifestation of that
idea. I couldn't, as you must recall, keep my hands, my
mouth, off them. Salt-sweet. Like not quite ripe strawberries covered with the light salt sweat of running
days and hopping, skipping, jumping hours.

The love of them—the touch, taste, and feel of
them—was not just an easy luxurious human vice;
they were, for me, A Thing To Do Instead. Instead of
Papa, instead of the Cloth, instead of Velma, and I
chose not to do without them. But I didn't go into the
church. At least I didn't do that. As to what I did do?
I told people I knew all about You. That I had received Your Powers. It was not a complete *lie;* but it
was a *complete* lie. I should never have, I admit, I
should never have taken their money in exchange for
well-phrased, well-placed, well-faced lies. But, mark
you, I hated it. Not for a moment did I love the lies
or the money.

But consider: The woman who left the hotel room.

Consider: The greentime, the noontime of the
archipelago.

Consider: Their hopeful eyes that were outdone only by their hoping breasts.

Consider: How I needed a comfortable evil to prevent my knowing what I could not bear to know.

Consider: How I hated and despised the money.

And now, consider: Not according to my just deserts, but according to *my* mercy, the little black girl that came a-looning at me today. Tell me, Lord, how could you leave a lass so long so lone that she could find her way to me? How could you? I weep for you, Lord. And it is because I weep for You that I had to do your work for You.

Do you know what she came for? Blue eyes. New, blue eyes, she said. Like she was buying shoes. "I'd like a pair of new blue eyes." She must have asked you for them for a very long time, and you hadn't replied. (A habit, I could have told her, a long-ago habit broken for Job—but no more.) She came to *me* for them. She had one of my cards. (Card enclosed.) By the way, I added the Micah—Elihue Micah Whitcomb. But I am called Soaphead Church. I cannot remember how or why I got the name. What makes one name more a person than another? Is the name the real thing, then? And the person only what his name says? Is that why to the simplest and friendliest of questions: "What is your name?" put to you by Moses, You would not say, and said instead "I am who I am." Like Popeye? I Yam What I Yam? Afraid you were, weren't you, to give out your name? Afraid they would know the name and then know you? Then they wouldn't fear you? It's quite all right. Don't be vexed. I mean no offense. I understand. I have been a bad man too, and an unhappy man too. But someday *I* will die. I was always so kind. Why do I have to die? The little girls. The little girls are the only things I'll miss. Do you know that when I touched their sturdy little tits and bit them—just a little—I felt I was being friendly? I didn't want to kiss their mouths or sleep in the bed with them or take a child bride for my own. Playful, I felt, and friendly. Not like the news-papers said. Not like the people whispered. And they didn't mind at all. Not at all. Remember how so many of them came back? No one would even try to under-stand that. If I'd been hurting them, would they have come back? Two of them, Doreen and Sugar Babe, they'd come together. I gave them mints, money, and they'd eat ice cream with their legs open while I played with them. It was like a party. And there wasn't nasti-ness, and there wasn't any filth, and there wasn't any odor, and there wasn't any groaning—just the light white laughter of little girls and me. And there wasn't any look—any long funny look—any long funny Velma look afterward. No look that makes you feel dirty afterward. That makes you want to die. With little girls it is all clean and good and friendly.

You have to understand that, Lord. You said, "Suf-fer little children to come unto me, and harm them not." Did you forget? Did you forget about the chil-dren? Yes. You forgot. You let them go wanting, sit on road shoulders, crying next to their dead mothers. I've seen them charred, lame, halt. You forgot, Lord. You forgot how and when to be God.

That's why I changed the little black girl's eyes for her, and I didn't touch her; not a finger did I lay on her. But I gave her those blue eyes she wanted. Not for pleasure, and not for money. I did what You did not, could not, would not do: I looked at that ugly little black girl, and I loved her. I played You. And it was a very good show!

I, I have caused a miracle. I gave her the eyes. I gave her the blue, blue, two blue eyes. Cobalt blue. A streak of it right out of your own blue heaven. No one else will see her blue eyes. But *she* will. And she will live happily ever after. I, I have found it meet and right so to do.

Now you are jealous. You are jealous of me.

You see? I, too, have created. Not aboriginally, like you, but creation is a heady wine, more for the taster than the brewer.

Having therefore imbibed, as it were, of the nectar, I am not afraid of You, of Death, not even of Life, and it's all right about Velma; and it's all right about Papa; and it's all right about the Greater and the Lesser Antilles. Quite all right. Quite.

With kindest regards, I remain,

Your,
Elihue Micah Whitcomb

Soaphead Church folded the sheets of paper into three equal parts and slipped them into an envelope. Although he had no seal, he longed for sealing wax. He removed a cigar box from under the bed and rummaged about in it. There were some of his most precious things: a sliver of jade that had dislodged from a cuff link at the Chicago hotel; a gold pendant shaped like a Y with a piece of coral attached to it that had belonged to the mother he never knew; four large hairpins that Velma had left on the rim of the bathroom sink; a powder blue grosgrain ribbon from the head of a little girl named Precious Jewel; a blackened faucet head from the sink in a jail cell in Cincinnati; two marbles he had found under a bench in Morningside Park on a very fine spring day; an old Lucky Hart catalog that smelled still of nut-brown and mocha face powder, and lemon vanishing cream. Distracted by his things, he forgot what he had been looking for. The effort to recall was too great; there was a buzzing in his head, and a wash of fatigue overcame him. He closed his box, eased himself out on the bed, and slipped into an ivory sleep from which he could not hear the tiny yelps of an old lady who had come out of her candy store and found the still carcass of an old dog named Bob.

Summer

I have only to break into the tightness of a strawberry, and I see summer—its dust and lowering skies. It remains for me a season of storms. The parched days and sticky nights are undistinguished in my mind, but the storms, the violent sudden storms, both frightened and quenched me. But my memory is uncertain; I recall a summer storm in the town where we lived and imagine a summer my mother knew in 1929. There was a tornado that year, she said, that blew away half of south Lorain. I mix up her summer with my own. Biting the strawberry, thinking of storms, I see her. A slim young girl in a pink crepe dress. One hand is on her hip; the other lolls about her thigh—waiting. The wind swoops her up, high above the houses, but she is still standing, hand on hip. Smiling. The anticipation and promise in her lolling hand are not altered by the holocaust. In the summer tornado of 1929, my mother's hand is unextinguished. She is strong, smiling, and relaxed while the world falls down about her. So much for memory. Public fact becomes private reality, and the seasons of a Midwestern town become the *Moirai* of our small lives.

The summer was already thick when Frieda and I received our seeds. We had waited since April for the magic package containing the packets and packets of seeds we were to sell for five cents each, which would entitle us to a new bicycle. We believed it, and spent a major part of every day trooping about the town selling them. Although Mama had restricted us to the homes of people she knew or the neighborhoods familiar to us, we knocked on all doors, and floated in and out of every house that opened to us: twelve-room houses that sheltered half as many families, smelling of grease and urine; tiny wooden four-room houses tucked into bushes near the railroad tracks; the up-over places—apartments up over fish markets, butcher shops, furniture stores, saloons, restaurants; tidy brick houses with flowered carpets and glass bowls with fluted edges.

During that summer of the seed selling we thought about the money, thought about the seeds, and listened with only half an ear to what people were saying. In the houses of people who knew us we were asked to come in and sit, given cold water or lemonade; and while we sat there being refreshed, the people continued their conversations or went about their chores. Little by little we began to piece a story together, a secret, terrible, awful story. And it was only after two or three such vaguely overheard conversations that we realized that the story was about Pecola. Properly placed, the fragments of talk ran like this:

"Did you hear about that girl?"

"What? Pregnant?"

"Yas. But guess who?"

"Who? I don't know all these little old boys."

"That's just it. Ain't no little old boy. They say it's Cholly."

"Cholly? Her daddy?"

"Uh-huh."

"Lord. Have mercy. That dirty nigger."

"'Member that time he tried to burn them up? I knew he was crazy for sure then."

"What's she gone do? The mama?"

"Keep on like she been, I reckon. He taken off."

"County ain't gone let her keep that baby, is they?"

"Don't know."

"None of them Breedloves seem right anyhow. That boy is off somewhere every minute, and the girl was always foolish."

"Don't nobody know nothing about them anyway. Where they come from or nothing. Don't seem to have no people."

"What you reckon make him do a thing like that?"

"Beats me. Just nasty."

"Well, they ought to take her out of school."

"Ought to. She carry some of the blame."

"Oh, come on. She ain't but twelve or so."

"Yeah. But you never know. How come she didn't fight him?"

"Maybe she did."

"Yeah? You never know."

"Well, it probably won't live. They say the way her mama beat her she lucky to be alive herself."

"She be lucky if it don't live. Bound to be the ugliest thing walking."

"Can't help but be. Ought to be a law: two ugly people doubling up like that to make more ugly. Be better off in the ground."

"Well, I wouldn't worry none. It be a miracle if it live."

Our astonishment was short-lived, for it gave way to a curious kind of defensive shame; we were embarrassed for Pecola, hurt for her, and finally we just felt sorry for her. Our sorrow drove out all thoughts of the new bicycle. And I believe our sorrow was the more intense because nobody else seemed to share it. They were disgusted, amused, shocked, outraged, or even excited by the story. But we listened for the one who would say, "Poor little girl," or, "Poor baby," but there was only head-wagging where those words should have been. We looked for eyes creased with concern, but saw only veils.

I thought about the baby that everybody wanted dead, and saw it very clearly. It was in a dark, wet place, its head covered with great O's of wool, the black face holding, like nickels, two clean black eyes, the flared nose, kissing-thick lips, and the living, breathing silk of black skin. No synthetic yellow bangs suspended over marble-blue eyes, no pinched nose and bowline mouth. More strongly than my fondness for Pecola, I felt a need for someone to want the black baby to live—just to counteract the universal love of white baby dolls, Shirley Temples, and Maureen Peals. And Frieda must have felt the same thing. We did not think of the fact that Pecola was not married; lots of girls had babies who were not married. And we did not dwell on the fact that the baby's father was Pecola's father too; the process of having a baby by any male was incomprehensible to us—at least she knew her father. We thought only of this overwhelming hatred for the unborn baby. We remembered Mrs. Breedlove knocking Pecola down and soothing the pink tears of the frozen doll baby that sounded like the door of our icebox. We remembered the knuckled eyes of schoolchildren under the gaze of Meringue Pie and the eyes of these same children when they looked at Pecola. Or maybe we didn't remember; we just knew. We had defended ourselves since memory against everything and everybody, considered all speech a code to be broken by us, and all gestures subject to careful analysis; we had become headstrong, devious and arrogant. Nobody paid us any attention, so we paid very good attention to ourselves. Our limitations were not known to us—not then. Our only handicap was our size; people gave us orders because they were bigger and stronger. So it was with confidence, strengthened by pity and pride, that we decided to change the course of events and alter a human life.

"What we gone do, Frieda?"

"What can we do? Miss Johnson said it would be a miracle if it lived."

"So let's make it a miracle."

"Yeah, but how?"

"We could pray."

"That's not enough. Remember last time with the bird?"

"That was different; it was half-dead when we found it."

"I don't care, I still think we have to do something really strong this time."

"Let's ask Him to let Pecola's baby live and promise to be good for a whole month."

"O.K. But we better give up something so He'll know we really mean it this time."

"Give up what? We ain't got nothing. Nothing but the seed money, two dollars."

"We could give that. Or, you know what? We could give up the bicycle. Bury the money and . . . plant the seeds."

"All of the money?"

"Claudia, do you want to do it or not?"

"O.K. I just thought . . . O.K."

"We have to do it *right*, now. We'll bury the money over by her house so we can't go back and dig it up, and we'll plant the seeds out back of our house so we can watch over them. And when they come up, we'll know everything is all right. All right?"

"All right. Only let me sing this time. You say the magic words."

LOOKLOOKHERECOMESAFRIENDTHE
FRIENDWILLPLAYWITHJANETHEYWI
LLPLAYAGOODGAMEPLAYJANEPLAY

*How many times a minute are you going to look inside that
old thing?*

I didn't look in a long time.

You did too—

So what? I can look if I want to.

*I didn't say you couldn't. I just don't know why you have
to look every minute. They aren't going anywhere.*

I know it. I just like to look.

You scared they might go away?

Of course not. How can they go away?

The others went away.

They didn't go away. They changed.

Go away. Change. What's the difference?

A lot. Mr. Soaphead said they would last forever.

Forever and ever Amen?

Yes, if you want to know.

You don't have to be so smarty when you talk to me.

I'm not being smarty. You started it.

I'd just like to do something else besides watch you stare in that mirror.

You're just jealous.

I am not.

You are. You wish you had them.

Ha. What would I look like with blue eyes?

Nothing much.

If you're going to keep this up, I may as well go on off by myself.

No. Don't go. What you want to do?

We could go outside and play, I guess.

But it's too hot.

You can take your old mirror. Put it in your coat pocket, and you can look at yourself up and down the street.

Boy! I never would have thought you'd be so jealous.

Oh, come on!

You are.

Are what?

Jealous.

O.K. So I'm jealous.

See. I told you.

No. I told you.

Are they really nice?

Yes. Very nice.

Just "very nice"?

Really, truly, very nice.

Really, truly, bluely nice?

Oh, God. You are crazy.

I am not!

I didn't mean it that way.

Well, what did you mean?

Come on. It's too hot in here.

Wait a minute. I can't find my shoes.

Here they are.

Oh. Thank you.

Got your mirror?

Yes dearie. . . .

Well, let's go then. . . . Ow!

What's the matter?

The sun is too bright. It hurts my eyes.

Not mine. I don't even blink. Look. I can look right at the sun.

Don't do that.

Why not? It doesn't hurt. I don't even have to blink.

Well, blink anyway. You make me feel funny, staring at the sun like that.

Feel funny how?

I don't know.

Yes, you do. Feel funny how?

I told you, I don't know.

Why don't you look at me when you say that? You're looking drop-eyed like Mrs. Breedlove.

Mrs. Breedlove look drop-eyed at you?

Yes. Now she does. Ever since I got my blue eyes, she look away from me all of the time. Do you suppose she's jealous too?

Could be. They are pretty, you know.

I know. He really did a good job. Everybody's jealous. Every time I look at somebody, they look off.

Is that why nobody has told you how pretty they are?

Sure it is. Can you imagine? Something like that happening to a person, and nobody but nobody saying anything about it? They all try to pretend they don't see them. Isn't that funny? . . . I said, isn't that funny?

Yes.

You are the only one who tells me how pretty they are.

Yes.

You are a real friend. I'm sorry about picking on you before. I mean, saying you were jealous and all.

That's all right.

No. Really. You are my very best friend. Why didn't I know you before?

You didn't need me before.

Didn't need you?

I mean . . . you were so unhappy before. I guess you didn't notice me before.

I guess you're right. And I was so lonely for friends. And you were right here. Right before my eyes.

No, honey. Right after your eyes.

What?

What does Maureen think about your eyes?

She doesn't say anything about them. Has she said anything to you about them?

No. Nothing.

Do you like Maureen?

Oh. She's all right. For a half-white girl, that is.

I know what you mean. But would you like to be her friend? I mean, would you like to go around with her or anything?

No.

Me neither. But she sure is popular.

Who wants to be popular?

Not me.

Me neither.

But you couldn't be popular anyway. You don't even go to school.

You don't either.

I know. But I used to.

What did you stop for?

They made me.

Who made you?

I don't know. After that first day at school when I had my blue eyes. Well, the next day they had Mrs. Breedlove come out. Now I don't go anymore. But I don't care.

You don't?

No, I don't. They're just prejudiced, that's all.

Yes, they sure are prejudiced.

Just because I got blue eyes, bluer than theirs, they're prejudiced.

That's right.

They are bluer, aren't they?

Oh, yes. Much bluer.

Bluer than Joanna's?

Much bluer than Joanna's.

And bluer than Michelena's?

Much bluer than Michelena's.

I thought so. Did Michelena say anything to you about my eyes?

No. Nothing.

Did you say anything to her?

No.

How come?

How come what?

How come you don't talk to anybody?

I talk to you.

Besides me.

I don't like anybody besides you.

Where do you live?

I told you once.

What is your mother's name?

Why are you so busy meddling me?

I just wondered. You don't talk to anybody. You don't go to school. And nobody talks to you.

How do you know nobody talks to me?

They don't. When you're in the house with me, even Mrs. Breedlove doesn't say anything to you. Ever. Sometimes I wonder if she even sees you.

Why wouldn't she see me?

I don't know. She almost walks right over you.

Maybe she doesn't feel too good since Cholly's gone.

Oh, yes. You must be right.

She probably misses him.

I don't know why she would. All he did was get drunk and beat her up.

Well, you know how grown-ups are.

Yes. No. How are they?

Well, she probably loved him anyway.

HIM?

Sure. Why not? Anyway, if she didn't love him, she sure let him do it to her a lot.

That's nothing.

How do you know?

I saw them all the time. She didn't like it.

Then why'd she let him do it to her?

Because he made her.

How could somebody make you do something like that?

Easy.

Oh, yeah? How easy?

They just make you, that's all.

I guess you're right. And Cholly could make anybody do anything.

He could not.

He made you, didn't he?

Shut up!

I was only teasing.

Shut up!

O.K. O.K.

He just tried, see? He didn't do anything. You hear me?

I'm shutting up.

You'd better. I don't like that kind of talk.

I said I'm shutting up.

You always talk so dirty. Who told you about that, anyway?

I forget.

Sammy?

No. You did.

I did not.

You did. You said he tried to do it to you when you were sleeping on the couch.

See there! You don't even know what you're talking about. It was when I was washing dishes.

Oh, yes. Dishes.

By myself. In the kitchen.

Well, I'm glad you didn't let him.

Yes.

Did you?

Did I what?

Let him.

Now who's crazy?

I am, I guess.

You sure are.

Still . . .

Well. Go ahead. Still what?

I wonder what it would be like.

Horrible.

Really?

Yes. Horrible.

Then why didn't you tell Mrs. Breedlove?

I did tell her!

I don't mean about the first time. I mean about the second time, when you were sleeping on the couch.

I wasn't sleeping! I was reading!

You don't have to shout.

You don't understand anything, do you? She didn't even believe me when I told her.

So that's why you didn't tell her about the second time?

She wouldn't have believed me then either.

You're right. No use telling her when she wouldn't believe you.

That's what I'm trying to get through your thick head.

O.K. I understand now. Just about.

What do you mean, just about?

You sure are mean today.

You keep on saying mean and sneaky things. I thought you were my friend.

I am. I am.

Then leave me alone about Cholly.

O.K.

There's nothing more to say about him, anyway. He's gone, anyway.

Yes. Good riddance.

Yes. Good riddance.

And Sammy's gone too.

And Sammy's gone too.

So there's no use talking about it. I mean them.

No. No use at all.

It's all over now.

Yes.

And you don't have to be afraid of Cholly coming at you anymore.

No.

That was horrible, wasn't it?

Yes.

The second time too?

Yes.

Really? The second time too?

Leave me alone! You better leave me alone.

Can't you take a joke? I was only funning.

I don't like to talk about dirty things.

Me neither. Let's talk about something else.

What? What will we talk about?

Why, your eyes.

Oh, yes. My eyes. My blue eyes. Let me look again.

See how pretty they are.

Yes. They get prettier each time I look at them.

They are the prettiest I've ever seen.

Really?

Oh, yes.

Prettier than the sky?

Oh, yes. Much prettier than the sky.

Prettier than Alice-and-Jerry Storybook eyes?

Oh, yes. Much prettier than Alice-and-Jerry Storybook eyes.

And prettier than Joanna's?

Oh, yes. And bluer too.

Bluer than Michelena's?

Yes.

Are you sure?

Of course I'm sure.

You don't sound sure. . . .

Well, I am sure. Unless. . ? .

Unless what?

Oh, nothing. I was just thinking about a lady I saw yester-day. Her eyes sure were blue. But no. Not bluer than yours.

Are you sure?

Yes. I remember them now. Yours are bluer.

I'm glad.

Me too. I'd hate to think there was anybody around with bluer eyes than yours. I'm sure there isn't. Not around here, anyway.

But you don't know, do you? You haven't seen every-body, have you?

No. I haven't.

So there could be, couldn't there?

Not hardly.

But maybe. Maybe. You said "around here." Nobody "around here" probably has bluer eyes. What about some-place else? Even if my eyes are bluer than Joanna's and bluer than Michelena's and bluer than that lady's you saw, sup-pose there is somebody way off somewhere with bluer eyes than mine?

Don't be silly.

There could be. Couldn't there?

Not hardly.

But suppose. Suppose a long way off. In Cincinnati, say, there is somebody whose eyes are bluer than mine? Suppose there are *two* people with bluer eyes?

So what? You asked for blue eyes. You got blue eyes.
He should have made them bluer.
Who?
Mr. Soaphead.
Did you say what color blue you wanted them?
No. I forgot.
Oh. Well.
Look. Look over there. At that girl. Look at her eyes. Are they bluer than mine?
No, I don't think so.
Did you look real good?
Yes.
Here comes someone. Look at his. See if they're bluer.
You're being silly. I'm not going to look at everybody's eyes.
You have to.
No I don't.
Please. If there is somebody with bluer eyes than mine, then maybe there is somebody with the bluest eyes. The bluest eyes in the whole world.
That's just too bad, isn't it?
Please help me look.
No.
But suppose my eyes aren't blue enough?
Blue enough for what?
Blue enough for . . . I don't know. Blue enough for something. Blue enough . . . for you!
I'm not going to play with you anymore.
Oh. Don't leave me.
Yes. I am.
Why? Are you mad at me?
Yes.

Because my eyes aren't blue enough? Because I don't have the bluest eyes?

No. Because you're acting silly.

Don't go. Don't leave me. Will you come back if I get them?

Get what?

The bluest eyes. Will you come back then?

Of course I will. I'm just going away for a little while.

You promise?

Sure. I'll be back. Right before your very eyes.

So it was.

A little black girl yearns for the blue eyes of a little white girl, and the horror at the heart of her yearning is exceeded only by the evil of fulfillment.

We saw her sometimes. Frieda and I—after the baby came too soon and died. After the gossip and the slow wagging of heads. She was so sad to see. Grown people looked away; children, those who were not frightened by her, laughed outright.

The damage done was total. She spent her days, her tendril, sap-green days, walking up and down, up and down, her head jerking to the beat of a drummer so distant only she could hear. Elbows bent, hands on shoulders, she flailed her arms like a bird in an eternal, grotesquely futile effort to fly. Beating the air, a winged but grounded bird, intent on the blue void it could not reach—could not even see—but which filled the valleys of the mind.

We tried to see her without looking at her, and never, never went near. Not because she was absurd, or repulsive, or because we were frightened, but because we had failed her. Our flowers never grew. I was convinced that Frieda was right, that I had planted them too deeply. How could I have been so sloven? So we avoided Pecola Breedlove—forever.

And the years folded up like pocket handkerchiefs. Sammy left town long ago; Cholly died in the workhouse; Mrs. Breedlove still does housework. And Pecola is somewhere in that little brown house she and her mother moved to on the edge of town, where you can see her even now, once in a while. The birdlike gestures are worn away to a mere picking and plucking her way between the tire rims and the sunflowers, between Coke bottles and milkweed, among all the waste and beauty of the world—which is what she herself was. All of our waste which we dumped on her and which she absorbed. And all of our beauty, which was hers first and which she gave to us. All of us—all who knew her—felt so wholesome after we cleaned ourselves on her. We were so beautiful when we stood astride her ugliness. Her simplicity decorated us, her guilt sanctified us, her pain made us glow with health, her awkwardness made us think we had a sense of humor. Her inarticulateness made us believe we were eloquent. Her poverty kept us generous. Even her waking dreams we used—to silence our own nightmares. And she let us, and thereby deserved our contempt. We honed our egos on her, padded our characters with her frailty, and yawned in the fantasy of our strength.

And fantasy it was, for we were not strong, only aggressive; we were not free, merely licensed; we were not compassionate, we were polite; not good, but well behaved. We courted death in order to call ourselves brave, and hid like thieves from life. We substituted good grammar for intellect; we switched habits to simulate maturity; we rearranged lies and called it truth, seeing in the new pattern of an old idea the Revelation and the Word.

She, however, stepped over into madness, a madness which protected her from us simply because it bored us in the end.

Oh, some of us "loved" her. The Maginot Line. And Cholly loved her. I'm sure he did. He, at any rate, was the one who loved her enough to touch her, envelop her, give something of himself to her. But his touch was fatal, and the something he gave her filled the matrix of her agony with death. Love is never any better than the lover. Wicked people love wickedly, violent people love violently, weak people love weakly, stupid people love stupidly, but the love of a free man is never safe. There is no gift for the beloved. The lover alone possesses his gift of love. The loved one is shorn, neutralized, frozen in the glare of the lover's inward eye.

And now when I see her searching the garbage—for what? The thing we assassinated? I talk about how I did *not* plant the seeds too deeply, how it was the fault of the earth, the land, of our town. I even think now that the land of the entire country was hostile to marigolds that year. This soil is bad for certain kinds of flowers. Certain seeds it will not nurture, certain fruit it will not bear, and when the land kills of its own volition, we acquiesce and say the victim had no right to live. We are wrong, of course, but it doesn't matter. It's too late. At least on the edge of my town, among the garbage and the sunflowers of my town, it's much, much, much too late.

Afterword

We had just started elementary school. She said she wanted blue eyes. I looked around to picture her with them and was violently repelled by what I imagined she would look like if she had her wish. The sorrow in her voice seemed to call for sympathy, and I faked it for her, but, astonished by the desecration she proposed, I "got mad" at her instead.

Until that moment I had seen the pretty, the lovely, the nice, the ugly, and although I had certainly used the word "beautiful," I had never experienced its shock—the force of which was equaled by the knowledge that no one else recognized it, not even, or especially, the one who possessed it.

It must have been more than the face I was examining: the silence of the street in the early afternoon, the light, the atmosphere of confession. In any case it was the first time I knew beautiful. Had imagined it for myself. Beauty was not simply something to behold; it was something one could *do*.

The Bluest Eye was my effort to say something about that; to say something about why she had not, or possibly ever would have, the experience of what she possessed and also why she prayed for so radical an alteration. Implicit in her desire was racial self-loathing. And twenty years later I was still wondering about how one learns that. Who told her? Who made her feel that it was better to be a freak than what she was? Who had looked at her and found her so wanting, so small a weight on the beauty scale? The novel pecks away at the gaze that condemned her.

The reclamation of racial beauty in the sixties stirred these thoughts, made me think about the necessity for the claim. Why, although reviled by others, could this beauty not be taken for granted within the community? Why did it need wide public articulation to exist? These are not clever questions. But in 1962 when I began this story, and in 1965 when it began to be a book, the answers were not as obvious to me as they quickly became and are now. The assertion of racial beauty was not a reaction to the self-mocking, humorous critique of cultural/racial foibles common in all groups, but against the damaging internalization of assumptions of immutable inferiority originating in an outside gaze. I focused, therefore, on how something as grotesque as the demonization of an entire race could take root inside the most delicate member of society: a child; the most vulnerable member: a female. In trying to dramatize the devastation that even casual racial contempt can cause, I chose a unique situation, not a representative one. The extremity of Pecola's case stemmed largely from a crippled and crippling family—unlike the average black family and unlike the narrator's. But singular as Pecola's life was, I believed some aspects of her woundability were lodged in all young girls. In exploring the social and domestic aggression that could cause a child to literally fall apart, I mounted a series of rejections, some routine, some exceptional, some monstrous, all the while trying hard to avoid complicity in the demonization process Pecola was subjected to. That is, I did not want to dehumanize the characters who trashed Pecola and contributed to her collapse.

One problem was centering: the weight of the novel's inquiry on so delicate and vulnerable a character could smash her and lead readers into the comfort of pitying her rather than into an interrogation of themselves for the smashing. My solution—break the narrative into parts that had to be reassembled by the reader—seemed to me a good idea, the execution of which does not satisfy me now. Besides, it didn't work: many readers remain touched but not moved.

The other problem, of course, was language. Holding the despising glance while sabotaging it was difficult. The novel tried to hit the raw nerve of racial self-contempt, expose it, then soothe it not with narcotics but with language that replicated the agency I discovered in my first experience of beauty. Because that moment was so racially infused (my revulsion at what my school friend wanted: very blue eyes in a very black skin; the harm she was doing to *my* concept of the beautiful), the struggle was for writing that was indisputably black. I don't yet know quite what that is, but neither that nor the attempts to disqualify an effort to find out keeps me from trying to pursue it.

Some time ago I did the best job I could of describing strategies for grounding my work in race-specific yet race-free prose. Prose free of racial hierarchy and triumphalism. Parts of that description are as follows.

The opening phrase of the first sentence, "Quiet as it's kept," had several attractions for me. First, it was a familiar phrase, familiar to me as a child listening to adults; to black women conversing with one another, telling a story, an anecdote, gossip about some one or event within the circle, the family, the neighborhood. The words are conspiratorial. "Shh, don't tell anyone else," and "No one is allowed to know this." It is a secret between us and a secret that is being kept from us. The conspiracy is both held and withheld, exposed and sustained. In some sense it was precisely what the act of writing the book was: the public exposure of a private confidence. In order to comprehend fully the duality of that position, one needs to be reminded of the political climate in which the writing took place, 1965–69, a time of great social upheaval in the lives of black people. The publication (as opposed to the writing) involved the exposure; the writing was the disclosure of secrets, secrets "we" shared and those withheld from us by ourselves and by the world outside the community.

"Quiet as it's kept" is also a figure of speech that is written, in this instance, but clearly chosen for how speakerly it is, how it speaks and bespeaks a particular world and its ambience. Further, in addition to its "back fence" connotation, its suggestion of illicit gossip, of thrilling revelation, there is also, in the "whisper," the assumption (on the part of the reader) that the teller is on the inside, knows something others do not, and is going to be generous with this privileged information. The intimacy I was aiming for, the intimacy between the reader and the page, could start up immediately because the secret is being shared, at best, and eavesdropped upon, at the least. Sudden familiarity or instant intimacy seemed crucial to me. I did not want the reader to have time to wonder, "What do I have to do, to give up, in order to read this? What defense do I need, what distance maintain?" Because I know (and the reader does not—he or she has to wait for the second sentence) that this is a terrible story about things one would rather not know anything about.

What, then, is the Big Secret about to be shared? The thing we (reader and I) are "in" on? A botanical aberration. Pollution, perhaps. A skip, perhaps, in the natural order of things: a September, an autumn, a fall without marigolds. Bright, common, strong and sturdy marigolds. When? In 1941, and since that is a momentous year (the beginning of World War II for the United States), the "fall" of 1941, just before the declaration of war, has a "closet" innuendo. In the temperate zone where there is a season known as "fall" during which one expects marigolds to be at their peak, in the months before the beginning of U.S. participation in World War II, something grim is about to be divulged. The next sentence will make it clear that the sayer, the one who knows, is a child speaking, mimicking the adult black women on the porch or in the backyard. The opening phrase is an effort to be grown-up about this shocking information. The point of view of a child alters the priority an adult would assign the information. "We thought . . . it was because Pecola was having her father's baby that the marigolds did not grow" foregrounds the flowers, backgrounds illicit, traumatic, incomprehensible sex coming to its dreaded fruition. This forgrounding of "trivial" information and backgrounding of shocking knowledge secures the point of view but gives the reader pause about whether the voice of children can be trusted at all or is more trustworthy than an adult's. The reader is thereby protected from a confrontation too soon with the painful details, while simultaneously provoked into a desire to know them. The nov-

elty, I thought, would be in having this story of female
violation revealed from the vantage point of the victims or
could-be victims of rape—the persons no one inquired of
(certainly not in 1965): the girls themselves. And since the
victim does not have the vocabulary to understand the violence or its context, gullible, vulnerable girlfriends, looking
back as the knowing adults they pretended to be in the
beginning, would have to do that for her, and would have
to fill those silences with their own reflective lives. Thus, the
opening provides the stroke that announces something more
than a secret shared, but a silence broken, a void filled, an
unspeakable thing spoken at last. And it draws the connection between a minor destabilization in seasonal flora and
the insignificant destruction of a black girl. Of course
"minor" and "insignificant" represent the outside world's
view—for the girls, both phenomena are earthshaking
depositories of information they spend that whole year of
childhood (and afterward) trying to fathom, and cannot. If
they have any success, it will be in transferring the problem
of fathoming to the presumably adult reader, to the inner
circle of listeners. At the least they have distributed the
weight of these problematical questions to a larger constitu-
ency, and justified the public exposure of a privacy. If the
conspiracy that the opening words announce is entered into
by the reader, then the book can be seen to open with its
close: a speculation on the disruption of "nature" as being
a social disruption with tragic individual consequences in
which the reader, as part of the population of the text, is
implicated.

   However, a problem lies in the central chamber of the
novel. The shattered world I built (to complement what is

happening to Pecola), its pieces held together by seasons in childtime and commenting at every turn on the incompatible and barren white-family primer, does not in its present form handle effectively the silence at its center: the void that is Pecola's "unbeing." It should have had a shape—like the emptiness left by a boom or a cry. It required a sophistication unavailable to me, and some deft manipulation of the voices around her. She is not *seen* by herself until she hallucinates a self. And the fact of her hallucination becomes a kind of outside-the-book conversation.

Also, although I was pressing for a female expressiveness, it eluded me for the most part, and I had to content myself with female personae because I was not able to secure throughout the work the feminine subtext that is present in the opening sentence (the women gossiping, eager and aghast in "Quiet as it's kept"). The shambles this struggle became is most evident in the section on Pauline Breedlove, where I resorted to two voices, hers and the urging narrator's, both of which are extremely unsatisfactory to me. It is interesting to me now that where I thought I would have the most difficulty subverting the language to a feminine mode, I had the least: connecting Cholly's "rape" by the whitemen to his own of his daughter. This most masculine act of aggression becomes feminized in my language, "passive," and, I think, more accurately repellent when deprived of the male "glamour of shame" rape is (or once was) routinely given.

My choices of language (speakerly, aural, colloquial), my reliance for full comprehension on codes embedded in black culture, my effort to effect immediate co-conspiracy and intimacy (without any distancing, explanatory fabric), as well as my attempt to shape a silence while breaking it are attempts to transfigure the complexity and wealth of Black-American culture into a language worthy of the culture.

Thinking back now on the problems expressive language presented to me, I am amazed by their currency, their tenacity. Hearing "civilized" languages debase humans, watching cultural exorcisms debase literature, seeing oneself preserved in the amber of disqualifying metaphors—I can say that my narrative project is as difficult today as it was thirty years ago.

With very few exceptions, the initial publication of *The Bluest Eye* was like Pecola's life: dismissed, trivialized, misread. And it has taken twenty-five years to gain for her the respectful publication this edition is.

Princeton, New Jersey
November, 1993